The Object of His Affection

by

Donald Proffit

SYNTHETIC PROPHETIC

Library of Congress Control Number: 2024919711

SYNTHETIC PROPHETIC ⇌
Kingston, New York, USA
www.syntheticprophetic.com

ISBN: 979-8-9856091-9-6

"The heart has its reasons,
which reason knows nothing of."

—Blaise Pascal, *Pensées* (1670)

Prelude

La Péniche, once an unfinished attic for storing restaurant supplies, sat atop the nautically-themed neighborhood tavern, The Barge. The upstairs bar and downstairs pub shared the same name but in different languages. The owners thought a French name brought more class to the repurposed storage room. They chose a classic Parisian cabaret décor, creating a mini-Moulin Rouge ambiance. The space was just large enough for a parlor grand piano between five and six feet long, with seating for seven comfortably around it. If you didn't mind a snug fit, a couple more people could squeeze in. Depending on the song, its dynamics, and the performer, patrons could watch sound waves ripple around the ice cubes in their drinks. A small service bar for ordering drinks stood by the stairway entrance, and a few cocktail tables occupied the remaining available space. However, there was no room for a cancan chorus line. *C'est la vie.* Truth be told, La Péniche felt more like someone's family room than an upscale nightclub.

Viktoria Sinclair and her longtime accompanist, Wolfgang Adler, had just finished performing a particularly moving rendition of the old standard "Mean To Me." Viktoria's vocal delivery vividly conveyed the hurt and confusion of being mistreated by a lover, capturing the audience's attention with every note. The deep yearning to be respected by the one you love made the plea for change even more poignant. As the applause died down, they retreated to the tiny cocktail table against the wall behind the grand piano, as there was no backstage to retreat to between sets. Wolfgang looked like he had something to say, and at eighty-two years old, he seldom held back when something was on his mind.

"Viktoria, my dear, the time has come for me to step down. I've decided to retire as your accompanist effective immediately."

His words hung in the air, a duet of bittersweet resignation and heartfelt appreciation for their shared years. It was late May, and Memorial Day weekend was a week away, marking the start of the busy summer season at the Jersey Shore. Deep down, Viktoria understood and embraced Wolfgang's decision, but she was still caught off guard. She'd need a piano player to take Wolfgang's place immediately.

"Wolfie, you sweet man, I knew this day was coming, but still, such short notice. It's Friday night, and how will I ever go on tomorrow without a pianist?"

"I'm old, Vik. Everything I do and say is on short notice these days. You'll manage; you always do. You're a survivor."

They continued for a few more minutes, hugging and shedding a tear. Then, they parted ways. Wolfgang's words echoed in her mind, their weight unsettling her more than she cared to admit. With a determined sigh, she slipped on her coat, the fabric brushing against her fingers like a comforting reminder of the familiar. She needed clarity, a different perspective, and perhaps a touch of that unique insight only the Midnight Word could deliver.

The night's chill greeted her as she stepped outside, her thoughts swirling with anticipation and apprehension. She walked briskly through the dimly lit streets, the glow from sodium-vapor lamps casting eerie, elongated shadows that danced around her feet as if guiding her to the Midnight Word. This late-night coffee house was her destination, known for its open mic nights and the best cup of coffee at the Shore. A refuge for those looking to share or discover new poems and songs in front of a welcoming, nonjudgmental crowd, the Midnight Word was the perfect place to unwind after Wolfgang's emotional farewell.

As she entered the cozy venue, she was met with the aroma of brewing coffee and the smell of freshly baked cookies and pastries. Random chatter filled the air as college students, hipsters, older couples, artists, and poets mingled—many of whom had been coming to the spot for years and were affectionately referred to as Night Crawlers by the staff. The place opened each night at ten o'clock and closed at three in the morning, far from the typical nine-to-five operation. A small platform served as a stage, with just enough space for one person and a mic stand. Beside it stood an old upright piano, perpetually in need of tuning due to the ocean air that constantly enveloped its strings, leaving a faint, salty residue and causing them to corrode over time.

Viktoria was taken to a table for two near the stage as a young poet prepared to read his work. A few regulars waved and called to her as she passed. She ordered a black coffee and bran muffin and listened, folding and refolding her paper napkin as if trying to make an origami swan and failing with each attempt.

One of the servers, an outwardly optimistic figure with a welcoming smile, bounded onto the stage, microphone in hand. "All right, everyone, give it up for our next poet of the night! He's got a way with words that'll make you feel like you're right there on the shore with him. Please welcome the incredibly talented Sam!"

The young man hopped on stage, retrieved a folded, handwritten sheet of paper from his shirt pocket, took a deep breath, and began to speak.

"Hi, I'm Sam, and I will read a new poem. I hope you like it." Sam cleared his throat noisily and began.

"The moon gazes where ocean meets sand,
Soul fragments scatter by the wind's hand.
Waves whisper secrets each star holds,
Dreams and shadows meet as night unfolds.
Boardwalk lights flicker with memories past,
Footsteps fade like ghosts, shadows cast.
We stitch together fragments in forgiving light,
Each word, each song, shared in the night.
Listen to whispers, the shore's stories told,
In midnight's space, we find and hold.
In waves' rhythm, in our cries,
We find the strength to rise."

Finger snaps and silent cheers in hands raised and waved in the air rewarded the poet's efforts. As Viktoria snapped along with the audience, she noticed a familiar figure across the room: Misty Drizzle, her dear friend and drag sister, was already there, chatting animatedly with a group of artists.

Seeing Misty brought back memories of their first meeting at Midnight Word. It had been a special night, a drag queen open mic, where both had signed up to perform. Viktoria remembered how Misty had struggled with her enormous hoop skirt, which was broader in circumference than she was tall. The audience had loved Misty's quirky charm, and Viktoria had felt an instant connection to her. Inspired by Billie Burke's Glinda dress from *The Wizard of Oz*, Misty's attire looked comically out of place in the intimate coffeehouse setting. Instead of sparkly stars and glittery snow crystals, her dress looked like it had been caught in a downpour on a muggy summer night and never dried out. The overall effect was one of dampness, with drab-colored fabric scraps appliqued to the lower portion of the gown, creating the illusion of fuzzy, deep green and black mold interspersed with white and brown mildew, creeping up from the bottom hem. If Viktoria had to describe Misty's drag in one word, that word would be "moist." Rather than being named after a geographical compass direction like the good and evil witches of Oz, Misty held the infamous honor of being the Jersey Witch of Questionable Taste.

After they became friends, Viktoria and Misty decided to channel their love for drag and creativity into a new venture. They opened a drag accessories shop, The Flambroidery, in Asbury Park, where they catered to other drag queens, providing them with fabulous drag attire and offering elaborately designed T-shirts for people of all ages. A small sign in the window advertised, "We Sell Boas by the Yard," catching the eyes of passersby. On Saturday mornings, the shop buzzed excitedly as they hosted workshops for anyone interested in creating drag wear or accessorizing their outfits for fun and fashion.

Intrigued, Viktoria watched as the young queen finally managed to sit at a nearby table, looking flustered but relieved. Viktoria decided to introduce herself.

"Darling, that skirt is a force of nature all its own!"

Viktoria said with a welcoming smile as she approached. "I'm Viktoria Sinclair. Mind if I join you?"

The young queen looked up, her eyes wide with awe and relief. "Oh, thank you so much! I'm Misty Drizzle. It's my first time here, and I'm a bit nervous."

"Don't worry; we've all been there. Just remember to have fun," Viktoria said, sitting down. "That's the most important thing."

Viktoria, in turn, shared tales of her early days in the drag scene, her challenges, and how she had carved out a place for herself in the community. She smiled at the memory. That night at Midnight Word, she found a kindred spirit and formed a bond that would last a lifetime. Misty had become more than a friend; she was family. Their shared experiences and mutual support carried them through the ups and downs of their careers and personal lives.

As the young poet left the stage, a server jumped up, thanking the young man who'd just shared his work, and announced the next person on the list of performers for the night.

"Our next performer is a talented young pianist who will share an original piece with you tonight. So, all you Night Crawlers, let's give Billy Pine a warm Midnight Word welcome." Finger snaps and fluttering hands greeted the pianist as he sat at the piano.

Billy played passionately, his fingers dancing gracefully across the keys. The audience sat spellbound, and Viktoria immediately recognized that she had discovered her next accompanist. After Billy's performance, Viktoria waved him over to her table and gestured for him to sit.

"Can I get you anything, honey? A coffee, juice, anything?"

"No thanks, ma'am, I'm okay."

"You know, you are a marvelous pianist—so moving." Viktoria tapped the spot where her heart lived. "May I call you Billy, Billy?"

Billy was somewhat starstruck and honored to receive the legendary drag performer's attention, and the two began to talk. Billy shared his dream of pursuing a music career and spoke about his local school music teacher job. He confessed that he struggled to find the right opportunities for his original compositions to be heard.

And then Viktoria pounced.

Chapter 1

Billy Pine was halfway through his final set of the night when he finished up a carefree rendition of Fats Waller's " 'Taint Nobody's Bizness If I Do." Customers gathered around the old Steinway, their drinks and spare change resting on the piano's once pristine and highly polished ebony lid. Old water rings and cigarette burns like faded tattoos stood witness to years of abuse.

"Billy, dear, would you be so kind…." Viktoria Sinclair sat to his right at a small table. The netting fastened to the brim of her hat cast a lattice shadow across her eyes, adding an air of mystery but not quite veiling her age, which was, after all, what she'd hoped the get-up would achieve. She extended her hand, and Billy helped her to the stool beside the piano. He then returned to her table, grabbed her drink—a gin martini—and set it on the piano where she could reach it. Polite applause circled the piano as Viktoria grabbed the mic from its stand.

"I hope you all are enjoying your fabulous selves at our fabulous petite soiree and our fabulous and stunningly beautiful piano man, Mr. Billy Pine. Isn't he just lusciousness, boys and girls? And so talented, too." The applause grew louder as Viktoria gestured for Billy to stand and be acknowledged.

With his perfect good looks and beach boy tan, having

Billy sit at the piano and never play a single note would be enough for some guests. His sun-streaked surfer hair embodied a carefree and beachy vibe; tousled and layered, it extended beyond the ears but not so long that it touched his shoulders. But Billy wasn't like the laid-back, adventurous wave riders that floated aimlessly on boards a hundred yards offshore, waiting for the perfect wave, or huddled around a lit joint under the Beachside boardwalk, its glowing ember signaling others that a meeting was in progress. Nevertheless, Billy looked relaxed and effortlessly calm as he charmed the bar's patrons, most of whom had come to hear him play. Even his father, William Senior—Big Billy to everybody who knew him—would stop by early to offer his support and ensure he had an audience, not that that was ever necessary. By nine o'clock, the bar was packed with customers who stayed until the place closed at midnight.

When you combined his stellar piano skills, his ability to fully engage the crowd with his killer smile, and the hottest boy-next-door look you'll ever see, Billy never had to face an empty tip jar at the end of the night. And that was good because, surviving on his first year's teacher salary, he needed every cent to make ends meet over the summer months. Billy had insisted on renting his own place after college, not wanting to rely on his dad. He now lived in a small apartment above a garage, part of an old carriage house that had once been part of a wealthy family's sprawling estate. The property had been subdivided and repurposed, now accommodating a different class of people.

"But alas, dear friends, I have sad news to share." The audience fake gasped in unison. Viktoria raised a hand encased in a long, rhinestone-studded glove in her flowing, midnight blue satin gown that shimmered with every gesture. Her emerald green wide-brimmed hat with delicate netting as a veil added a striking contrast to her ensemble. "We're nearing the end of our fabulous evening together. Just a few more songs for you." Another gasp. She stood, her high heels clicking softly as she stepped forward, her gown catching the dim lights of the piano bar. "But don't feel sad because now's the perfect opportunity to order one last libation at the bar and cherish our remaining time together." And then cheers went up from the intimate crowd.

Billy vamped until Viktoria began crooning a tragically cheeky rendition of "Am I Blue," followed by a peppy "Get Happy" to chase away the melancholy sadness of the previous song. The crowd ate it up. Some sang along when they could remember the words and hummed when they couldn't.

Viktoria always sang a few songs during each set. When she wasn't at the mic, which was most of the time, Billy filled her silence with glorious renditions of cherished ballads, torch songs, upbeat tunes, and the occasional popular contemporary hit.

Billy noticed a man walking into the room, standing tall and athletic as if his physique had been honed by years of sports and physical activity. His caramel skin, smooth and flawless, contrasted starkly with his white jacket—a chef's coat, Billy thought. He looked like he'd just gotten off work. The man grabbed a drink at the bar and leaned against the wall next to the piano, his slightly lowered head exposing a cascade of tight, dark curls, short and neatly trimmed, with a few strands falling charmingly across his forehead.

Despite his prominent cheekbones and razor-sharp jawline lending him a regal look, he didn't seem happy. Billy felt tense as he studied the rugged glower on the man's face. He knew this guy with soulful brown eyes framed by long, thick lashes. It was Pierce Talon, a former high school classmate. Billy's initial tenseness at seeing him turned into agitation.

A customer vacated his seat at the far end of the piano and headed to the restroom. Billy watched as Pierce moved in and grabbed the open barstool; stealing it would be more accurate. As Billy played the piano, the customer next to Pierce spoke up.

"Hey, man, that's someone's seat. He's coming right back."

Pierce put down his drink and pushed the previous occupant's empty glass and car keys aside, deliberately forming a protective circle with his arms on the piano's lid, defending his newly claimed territory.

"Fuck off."

Billy thought that looks could kill as he observed the interaction between the two men. The other man scowled with a you-have-got-to-be-kidding-me expression at the stranger, grabbed the discarded keys, ceded the territory, and waited for his friend to return.

Pierce slumped, face cradled in his hands. Billy wondered what Pierce's problem was, why he treated a customer like that, and what he was doing wearing full kitchen gear on a Friday night in a piano bar. Then, as if noticing Billy for the first time, which Billy knew was not the case, Pierce raised his head and looked directly at him. That's when the other customer returned with a fresh drink, puzzled that his seat had been pirated.

Billy kept an eye on the situation as Pierce turned toward the former stool's occupant and glared while his companion pulled him by his sleeve and whispered something in his ear. Whatever he said, the friend backed away from Pierce, choosing to stand instead of fighting over the bar stool. It was for the best, Billy thought. La Péniche couldn't tolerate a bar brawl; it was too small. The only bouncer in the place was stationed downstairs by the door at The Barge, and he'd never make it up the stairs in time to help should fisticuffs arise between the two men—make that three.

Between songs, Billy turned toward Viktoria and asked, "Do you know that guy sitting at the end of the piano? That's Pierce Talon. I had a crush on him in high school. I thought he liked me because he was always flirting, but he flirted with everyone: boys, girls, and even the teachers. And right now, he won't take his eyes off me—the one in the white jacket."

"You mean that hot number in a chef's jacket looking like he might crawl across the piano and take a bite out of you? Uh-uh, I don't know him, Billy. I haven't seen him in here before. He looks like trouble, too pretty for his own good. It's best to ignore his stare."

Billy glanced at Pierce again. Pierce rattled the ice cubes in his glass and glanced at the clock above the bar. It was eleven thirty, and the last call for drinks would be in fifteen minutes.

"Let's wrap this up, Viktoria."

Viktoria turned to the audience.

"All right, loves, it's nearing the time to bid a fond farewell. Get your hankies out if you need them to dab at your tears. What? No hankies? Just grab a cocktail napkin, unfurl it, and get ready." Viktoria pulled a white handkerchief embroidered with purple pansies from her nonexistent cleavage, raised it high, and waved it to the crowd. The audience responded in kind, waving cocktail napkins above their heads.

Billy led off with an outrageous glissando culminating in a dominant seventh chord as Viktoria eyed the crowd and began singing "The Object of My Affection," a bouncy foxtrot from the 1930s that was always a crowd-pleaser, especially for the regulars. Viktoria always got the audience to sing along. She improvised a verse about how the object of her affection lived in a house of detention, which generated fits of uncontrollable laughter from the audience, especially from those who knew her, because it was true.

Billy remembered how Viktoria, instead of joining her drag sisters reading to children at the local library's drag queen story hour on Saturday mornings, decided she'd prefer reading stories to prisoners at the state prison. She'd only needed to volunteer once. She was an instant sensation, and the warden booked her for monthly readings. She even found a boyfriend, Wally, twenty years younger than her fifty-seven years. She was in heaven.

When the song ended, everyone clapped, and others cheered, "Yas, queen!" Then, Billy transitioned into their final number, a schmaltzy-waltzy rendition of "When I Grow Too Old To Dream."

Viktoria dabbed at make-believe tears, careful not to tangle her handkerchief in her store-bought lashes or smudge her makeup. She spoke the verse in her signature cigarette-scarred voice, campy and dirge-like, with just a hint of bitterness and regret that may not have been part of the act.

After the reminiscing verse about once being young, gay, and beautiful, she gestured to the audience to join her in lamenting about growing too old to dream and holding tight to the love that lived in their hearts. Some people interlocked arms and swayed; some raised their drinks in a toast, while others used their cellphones as torches.

What a way to bring down a crowd, but it worked every time. The customers applauded, paid their tabs, grabbed their belongings, and headed out into the night.

The place emptied quickly, and La Péniche always shut its doors promptly at midnight, leaving folks still feeling festive enough to make their way to the handful of other clubs that lined Ocean Boulevard and stayed open until 2:00 AM.

Billy packed up his music and split his tips with Viktoria; he was ready to leave. He noticed Pierce hadn't moved but just sat there watching.

"I'm going to talk to him."

"Be careful, Billy," Viktoria whispered in his ear as she passed him on her way to the stairs. "You tend to fall in love too easily, my dear boy, especially with those bad-boy types." Billy had had two short-term relationships with men who turned out to be no more than self-absorbed fuckboys, only in it for themselves. Billy wanted commitment, something that wasn't in their vocabulary. She winked, squeezed Billy's shoulders, kissed him, and disappeared down the stairs.

"Pierce Talon." Billy acknowledged the only remaining customer.

"Billy Pine, I haven't seen you in at least six years, since high school. I'd remember your gorgeous face anywhere."

The man was beautiful, the kind of beauty that could take you to better places: better jobs, better houses in better neighborhoods, better sex, anything you wanted or would want others to do for or to you.

Pierce gulped down the rest of his drink and forcefully slid the empty glass across the piano lid. It skidded to a stop against Billy's empty tip jar, a large brandy sifter, nearly knocking it to the floor. He got off the stool and stood before Billy. He was a couple of inches taller and ten to twenty pounds heavier than Billy.

The face that had seemed filled with troublesome thoughts just a few seconds before was instantly transformed as his smile stretched from sexy dimple to dimple. He grabbed the piano player, pulled him into a fierce hug, and held on for a moment too long, a moment that could have been uncomfortable if it hadn't been for how attractive Pierce was.

Billy's heart raced as he clung to Pierce; the sensation of their bodies pressed together sent a rush of heat through him. His cheeks flushed as he felt the bulk and definition of muscle pressing firmly against him. The guy was a beast, a beautiful beast, even with the remnant odors of whatever he had prepared for dinner embedded in his chef's coat.

Billy pulled away, momentarily flustered, his mind reeling from the unexpected intensity of the hug and the undeniable allure of Pierce's presence. Despite his intentions, he found himself admiring the rugged charm and athleticism exuding from Pierce, stirring up a whirlwind of emotions. Pierce Talon had been a star athlete in high school, state ice hockey champ, and all-around big man on campus. They weren't close, never best friends. They were in a couple of classes together. Billy remembered they'd been lab partners for a biology class project once. What had kept them from being friends seemed to be the crowd Pierce hung out with. Pierce always acted friendly toward Billy in class, but then in the hallways was aloof and cruel when he walked with his too-cool-for-school buddies.

Billy had always wondered what lay beneath the veneer of Pierce's charismatic smile and one-in-a-million good looks, and in this moment he wondered anew. Why had he acted so rude with the other customer? Maybe he was having a bad night. He had looked upset earlier.

"Hi, Pierce."

"Hiya, pal, long time, no see. You still live in town with your pops, or are you just visiting?"

"No, I live here in Beachside. I play here every night, except Mondays, and spend my days working on music and composing." Music was everything to Billy; he hoped to be discovered one day, not for fame, but for the chance to share his music with others. "What about you?"

"I graduated from culinary school in Manhattan a year ago. I've got a killer chef job lined up starting in the fall at one of the city's best eateries. It's in the theater district. I'm so psyched, but right now, I'm the chef at the Sea Spray Inn. Just for the season."

"Congrats, Pierce!" Billy thought about Pierce's behavior and bothered look earlier in the night and softened his stance. "Can I ask you something?"

"Sure thing, bud."

"You seemed pretty upset tonight. Why the sad face? Is everything okay?"

Billy placed his hand on Pierce's upper arm in a gesture of concern but questioned his action when the sensations from their earlier embrace flared up inside him again.

"Oh, that. Yeah, I was upset. My line cook, who handles the breakfast service at the hotel, walked out on me this morning. I don't see how I can manage it all on my own. I'll need to find someone to take over the breakfast service so I can focus on dinner and my nightly chef's special."

"I'm sure you'll be able to find someone, Pierce. A teacher or a college kid on summer break and looking for work."

Billy stooped to pick up his messenger bag, slung it over his shoulder, and headed toward the stairs. "Nice seeing you again, Pierce."

"Hey, wait a minute, Billy Boy. I've got an idea. Maybe you can help me out. Do me a big favor."

Billy stood silent, wondering what on earth Pierce could want from him.

"Billy, you could cook for me. Pick up the breakfast service until I can find a replacement."

Billy considered the request. It was outrageous and unexpected. "Sorry, Pierce. I would love to help you, but my days are for composing and practicing, and besides, I can't cook." Billy could cook. He liked cooking for his friends, and they enjoyed his food. But would he enjoy cooking for hotel guests? He thought that was a whole different story: a lot of pressure.

"Can you make eggs? How about French toast? Easy stuff, and I'll be there to help you out until you learn the ropes. You also get a season pass to Ocean Point Beach and a room to crash in behind the hotel in the staff barracks. So come on, help an old friend out."

Old friend? God lord! But Billy thought about it. He wanted his days for composing but could also use the extra money. As a struggling musician, he barely got by on his small salary and tips from the piano gig at La Péniche. And his next big paycheck wouldn't come until he returned to the classroom in September. Maybe he could make the time if it gave him some wiggle room with his finances. And besides, how difficult could it be for him to make breakfast for a few people at an old seaside hotel? He could manage this, maybe, especially if Pierce found someone for the job soon; it'd be over before he knew, and he'd have some cash in his pocket. The beach pass was a bonus, especially because Ocean Point Beach was exclusive to town residents and hotel guests only. No outsiders allowed.

"OK, I'll do it, but you've got to promise me you'll be there to show me the ropes, teach me what to do." Billy surprised himself with his impulsive response. Maybe it was the money. Or perhaps it was that killer smile.

"Thank you, Billy. I owe you, buddy."

"I'm not your buddy, not yet. We were former classmates at best. I'll do this because I could use the extra cash."

"Hey, a piano in the hotel lobby sits untouched all day. I'll check with Ron Service, the hotel manager, but I'm sure he'll let you use it when you're done in the kitchen. Think of it as a bonus for helping me out."

To work on a bigger and better piano rather than the beat-up blond Baldwin that had been surplused by the school district and for which he had paid only fifty dollars—would be a bonus. This may work out after all, Billy thought.

"When can you begin?" Pierce slipped back into his troubled look.

"How about tomorrow?"

Relief washed over Pierce's face, and he smiled. God, Billy thought, how could anyone have a smile that perfect? Pierce leaned in and gripped Billy in another hug, deeper this time and closer, like he was trying to pin Billy against the side of the piano, attempting to get him to submit, to tap out. But he couldn't tap out with his arms pinned to his ribcage. So, all Billy could do was hold on until he was released.

When the hug ended, Billy gasped for air and adjusted his clothing. Pierce swaggered to the door with his smile still in place. He seemed to be glowing, or was he gloating?

"See you tomorrow, Billy Boy. Let's aim for seven. Breakfast runs from eight until ten. I'll show you the ropes on your first day, and then you're on your own. You know where it is—the hotel's been in the same spot for the last hundred years."

Both men had grown up here. Pierce's family lived in Ocean Point, the next town down the coast from Beachside. Ocean Boulevard ran through both towns, north to south, and they shared the same high school, Beachside-Ocean Point High.

"I'll be there by seven. Thanks, Pierce, for the opportunity."

"Don't thank me; you're saving my ass, buddy-boy. You have no idea."

With that, Pierce bolted down the stairs to the parking lot.

Billy followed but took the door to his right instead of exiting outside at the bottom landing. He passed through the bar at The Barge, just off Ocean Boulevard and a block from the sea. The bar was located just within the town line of Beachside on the border with Ocean Point. Beachside was known for its classic boardwalk lined with arcades, fortune tellers, T-shirt shops, pizza stands, and rundown beachfront vacation rentals. On the other hand, Ocean Point was an exclusive enclave with large, weathered summer homes—mansions, really—designed to look like quaint seaside cottages for the gentry class.

He said goodnight to the staff and went to the manager's office, tucked away in a corner of the storeroom. The cramped and dimly lit office was an afterthought in the sprawling back area that housed the walk-in refrigerator. The musty smell of old receipts mixed with the sharp, salty smell of mussels and tiny clams stacked in sacks just outside the door. The manager was engulfed with checking inventory against a list pinched to a clipboard.

"Hi, Gus, I just want to get my pay."

Gus didn't turn around but raised one hand, a gesture Billy assumed meant that he was free to rummage through the desk on his own.

The manager's desk was chaotic, covered in a haphazard pile of papers, invoices, and various windowed envelopes. Billy sifted through the stack, the damp, greasy edges of some envelopes sticking to his fingers. Finally, he found his paycheck, its familiar shape and weight a small comfort in the disorder. As he pocketed his earnings, Billy glanced around at the cluttered space, taking in the flickering fluorescent light that cast eerie shadows on the walls lined with boxes of perishable goods. The low hum of the refrigerator added to the dreariness that permeated the room.

With a final nod to the manager, who was too absorbed in cataloging cans of condensed milk to notice, Billy stepped out of the office, eager to leave the rank-smelling confines behind. He crossed the storeroom, careful to avoid the puddles forming on the cracked linoleum floor, and pushed open the back door. The cool night air greeted him as he stepped outside, a welcome relief from the stagnant air inside.

Once outside, he unchained his bike and began pedaling the few short blocks to his apartment on Maple Avenue. The streets were quiet, the usual hustle of Beachside now replaced by a calm serenity. As he biked, Billy's thoughts drifted back to his encounter with Pierce earlier in the day. The offer of a cook's job at the Sea Spray Inn had seemed too good to be true, and that bear hug from Pierce had felt less like an embrace and more like a game of the hunter and the hunted.

He recalled a few incidents of teasing and bullying that had gone too far—stories from high school friends about two of Pierce's teammates. Billy had even been targeted briefly by those boys, and the emotional scars from those encounters still lingered. Pierce had never seemed to participate directly, but he was always there, a silent observer. Billy wondered if people really could change, if Pierce had changed. He wanted to believe it, but doubt gnawed at him.

Instead of taking the direct route home, Billy rode along River Road through the old neighborhood where he grew up, where his father still lived. His childhood home stood sentinel, a beacon of a safe harbor and his home port. A lamp in his father's bedroom was still on, casting dappled yellow light through the large front yard maple. The sight echoed recollections, both comforting and painful.

Then, the memory surfaced like an unexpected seizure, intense, uncontrollable, and disorienting. He pulled off the road onto the grassy verge by the river. Billy had always found solace in the river, a constant in his ever-changing life. The serene flow of water, weaving around large rocks—barely submerged obstacles to avoid or navigate around—mirrored his struggles and resilience. Growing up in Beachside, nestled between the river's edge and the ocean's shoreline, Billy had learned early on to find peace in nature's serenity.

He let the bike fall to the ground and stepped closer to the river's edge. A chill coursed through his body, and tears ran down his face. He stood in silence, glancing across the river to a different time: the winter of his senior year in high school.

Chapter 2

The river made its home on a shale bed. Water-worn boulders sculpted over thousands of years by the eternal current, especially those rising above the surface like polished stones, appeared deliberately placed to harmonize with the surrounding landscape. They generated endless eddies, their gurgles joining birdsongs and the wind in a natural symphony. The visual effect, particularly on a calm day when sections of the river were glasslike, reminded Billy of a manicured Japanese Zen water garden.

The river flowed along clay banks and emptied into a small inlet, its head adorned with tiny cottages like a quaint rustic tiara. In the middle of winter, the ice would arrive as if it had no relationship to the river on which it rested, separate and of its own mind, trapping the water below as it ran toward the bay and out to sea.

The tides wreaked havoc on the ice, especially along the banks where the inlet narrowed, allowing tidal forces to dominate the brackish water. The ice seemed to speak here, its chorus of creaks and cracks echoing through the night like a pubescent boy's voice, amplified under the full moon. This was when local red foxes would venture forth, daring to traverse the jagged shoreline and cross the river to the opposite bank. The daily temperatures and fluctuating tides pestered the ice, ratcheting, heaving, and jacking sharp shards skyward along the frozen edge. At the same time, beneath the crust, the unseen river maneuvered around rocks, fallen trees, and debris, constantly coursing toward its destiny, the Atlantic. The ice was born of the river and would return come spring. Still, for now, both were separate entities unless a circumstance would call them to work their menacing magic together, one pulling and the other tugging in common.

Yet, just a few hundred yards upstream, the river was lake-like, where the current moved swiftly along the bottom, leaving the surface untouched by ripples and eddies. On the coldest days, that frozen expanse of river was a popular spot for ice skating and pick-up hockey games among the locals.

Billy vividly remembered one cold winter afternoon with his dog, Finn, when he was a high school senior—a day that marked the first of two haunting events occurring just a week apart. Despite his desperate attempts to suppress these memories, they would creep back into his thoughts and dreams when least expected.

Although the painful memories haunted him, Billy cherished happier times with Finn. He recalled one summer evening when he and his father had taken Finn to the beach. The sky was painted with hues of orange and pink as the sun set. Billy threw a frisbee, and Finn dashed across the sand, leaping gracefully to catch it midair. His father, Big Billy, laughed heartily, his stern exterior momentarily softened by pure joy. After their game of disc toss, they sat together on a blanket, Finn nestled between them, her head resting on Billy's lap as they watched the waves crash gently against the shore. In those moments, Billy felt at peace and contented, his bond with Finn and his father growing ever stronger.

He also remembered how his father's grief was buried beneath a hardened exterior after his wife's—Billy's mother's—tragic death in a car accident when Billy was in eighth grade, a loss that had shattered both their worlds. Big Billy seldom spoke of his late wife, choosing instead to channel his pain into caring for Billy. A former navy officer, he believed in the power of resilience and the healing touch of companionship.

Recognizing the depth of Billy's sorrow, he had taken him to the local animal shelter three months after his mother died, hoping Billy could find an affinity with one of the deserving animals waiting to be adopted. As they wandered through the rows of hopeful eyes and wagging tails, Billy passed a kennel crate labeled with Finn's name. A sleek black Lab bounded forward when he glanced inside, tail wagging furiously.

It was as if Finn picked him out rather than Billy choosing a dog; an instant bond was forged. Big Billy asked his son if Finn was the one. Billy nodded, cuddling the dog close to his chest, the Lab's wet black snout nuzzling his throat.

"Billy," his dad said, his voice cracking slightly, "let's take Finn; she's here to help us heal."

But right now, standing on the riverbank, he found himself in the winter of his senior year, recalling the time he and his loyal black Labrador retriever had gone to the river for some skating before sunset.

Billy noticed three towering figures, Jake, Karl, and Pierce, clad in hockey gear, emerging from the shadows as he skated. Their blades cut through the ice with an intimidating rhythm—notorious ice hockey players from Beachside-Ocean Point High, known for their aggressive playing style on the rink and their penchant for bullying off of it. He bent down to reassure Finn with a pat on the head, but he lost his balance and ended up on all fours.

Billy recalled how one or two of his friends had had trouble with some of Pierce's hockey teammates during senior year. They called themselves The Posse and could make the school's hallways a living hell for kids perceived to be weaker, unpopular, or gay. Billy had been spared any interaction with the trio because Pierce had always been cordial towards him in classrooms and hallways, maybe oddly protective. Yet, he wondered what role Pierce had played in those altercations. Was he tagging along with the other two boys out of friendship, or was something more sinister at play? Maybe it was how he was raised, but Billy believed it was always best to forgive and move past misunderstandings and misdirected animosities. That seemed to be his modus operandi; he either held no grudges, was too forgiving, or continuously turned the other cheek when confronted by people out to do him harm. He had always given Pierce the benefit of the doubt as Pierce never seemed directly involved with harassing other kids, even though he always seemed to be there when The Posse found a target to abuse like he was now. A warning issued by his amygdala crawled across the lower third of his brain like a news ticker: THREAT DETECTED.

Karl spotted Billy and Finn on the ice. A mischievous grin spread across his face as he nudged his teammates, who eagerly joined him in targeting the unsuspecting duo.

"Hey, look at this loser! Can't even stand up straight. He's on all fours, just like his pathetic excuse for a dog!" Jake's words were laced with venom, dripping with the same disdain that permeated his actions.

"How's that feel, faggot?" Karl joined Jake's verbal attack, their voices a cacophony of cruelty reverberating across the frozen river.

Billy clenched his jaw, refusing to give them the satisfaction of seeing him falter further, even as their insults stung like salt in an open wound. He got into a crouch, one skate on the ice, but still unbalanced. He struggled to right himself and keep hold of Finn's leash.

For her part, Finn had been watching the entire scene with growing concern. As the threat grew, the black Lab's protective instincts kicked in. With a deep growl, Finn positioned herself between Billy and the aggressors, her fur raised and bristling in defiance.

As the situation escalated, one of the boys, Pierce, noticed the dog's defensive stance and hesitated momentarily. Billy couldn't tell if Pierce was just afraid of Finn or if he was concerned with their victim's wellbeing.

Pierce's face softened slightly as he stepped forward and lowered his hockey stick. "Come on, guys, let's leave him alone. It's not worth it," he said, his voice lacking conviction but still trying to defuse the situation. Jake and Karl turned to Pierce, their expressions a fusion of surprise and annoyance.

"What's wrong with you, Pierce? Are you going soft on us?" Karl sneered, giving Pierce a light shove.

Pierce glanced at Billy and then back at his friends, the inner conflict evident in his eyes. "Just... let's go. It's freezing out here," he mumbled, trying to sound authoritative while struggling to maintain control.

Karl and Jake exchanged looks before reluctantly nodding. "Whatever, man. Let's get out of here," Jake grumbled as the trio indulged in a round of exaggerated bro-slaps, their attempts to outdo each other looking more like a clumsy dance of backside assault.

Grateful for Finn's unwavering loyalty, Billy scrambled for secure footing and stood tall beside his faithful companion. A resilient spirit took hold of Billy as he rose against the cold cruelty that cracked the winter afternoon.

In the face of Finn's protective stance and Billy's new-found determination, the trio continued their retreat, their laughter fading into the distance. Billy skated to the shoreline, sat down to remove his skates, and headed home.

Billy and Finn went for a walk a week later—a day that would change Billy's life forever—on a bright Saturday morning with winter skies so sunny blue that it hurt to look up. It was the kind of day when Canadian geese kept to themselves on the snow-covered island midstream or in the few open patches of water near the shore, their heads tucked into feathers for protection against the cold. There was little space for paddling in the shallows as the ice had reclaimed most openings during the night. Occasionally, a rare break in the ice floe exposed the dark water beneath, too small to accommodate more than one or two geese, let alone a gaggle.

Life on the street that morning was reluctant to start, except for the steam and smoke rising from flues and pipes along the rooflines. Billy loved these morning walks with Finn. He noticed other dogs and their owners walking in twos, resembling old couples happy to be together. Some pairs would meet up with neighbors along the way, storm doors opening as dogs and their humans joined the fray of barks and gossip. On the street, their yaps and stories rose on breaths of escaping water vapors condensing into clouds of ice crystals, their woofs and words ascending like souls into heaven.

Billy walked toward the river; Finn insisted on getting closer to a break in the ice where two geese foraged, heads bobbing below the surface, tearing up any vegetation on the bottom. The dog pulled on her leash, and Billy tugged to balance the force, holding tightly to the lead. He wanted to give in to his dog's need to explore, even if it meant climbing down the bank, even if it was against his better judgment, even while the ice groaned and water splashed up and out of the opening at the river's edge.

Billy eased down the incline pulled by Finn. But when Finn's momentum increased, Billy's feet skimmed over the gravel as he tried to maintain control. The riverbank lacked the rungs of vines and weeds that, from May to November, would have kept him upright and given him traction. His grasp remained on the leash as he slid closer to the river. Finn moved to the break in the ice, her front legs straddling the opening and her rear legs safely planted on land. As Labs are wont to do, she nosed around in the water that bubbled up and over the icy rim of the hole, nibbling at it as it hit the air.

At that moment, Billy's momentum and forward movement seized control, causing him to fall. He was tossed the rest of the way until he landed on the narrow patch of land at the shoreline. In that final tumble, he lost grip of the leash, which fell from his hand and lay loose on the ground behind the dog.

"Finn," Billy called out, his voice strident and cracking. Finn continued to bite at the cold water fountains leaping up from the hole. Billy called out again. As the dog turned toward him to see what the fuss was about, the ice where her paws stood gave way, causing her head and upper body to fall into the river. As Billy crawled toward the leash in a desperate effort to grab it and pull Finn to safety, the break widened, and water rose like a plow, pushing the dog deeper and under the ice as her rear legs gave out, no match for the current beneath the ice. Billy panicked as the leash skipped across the ice and disappeared from view.

Billy regained his ground and rushed to the edge, only able to make out the silhouette of his dog looking up at him as she tried in vain to swim against the river's force and return to the opening in the ice. He continued to run along the water's edge, following the ghostly outline of his dog as she moved downstream, hoping against hope that there'd be another opening, another opportunity for escape, a chance for them to return home, to sit together in front of the fireplace, to be warm and dry, to anticipate the spring.

As Billy raced along the water's edge, he called for help, anyone, a neighbor, to help him save his dog. But the first responders he heard delivered a barrage of catcalls and taunts from the bank's top. Karl, Jake, and Pierce followed Billy in a parallel path at the riverbank's top, their skates hanging by tied laces slung over shoulders like saddlebags. Billy glanced up, pleading. Maybe they couldn't hear him. But then Billy noticed what looked like concern on Pierce's face, if only fleetingly. Pierce turned toward his friends. He was saying something to them and then looked back down toward Billy. Karl and Jake shrugged him off, pulled Pierce back into their group, and walked away from the riverbank.

By the time Billy turned back toward the river, Finn was gone, sluicing away around indifferent river rocks, into the inlet, and out to sea.

Chapter 3

Pierce was relieved that Billy took the job, sparing him from running the kitchen from sunup to sundown alone. He stared at the ceiling in the coolness of his spacious bedroom at his family's seaside house in Ocean Point. The room, usually a sanctuary with its deep blue walls, large windows offering an expansive ocean view, and plush cream-colored carpet, felt suffocating tonight. His mind drifted back to the incident he regretted most during high school: the morning he could have helped Billy but did nothing.

He repeatedly replayed the scene in his mind, recalling how Billy ran alongside the river, chasing Finn, who was visible through the thick lens of ice. The dog's fur spread out in the cold water like the delicate, waving tentacles of a no longer sessile sea anemone, creating an eerie aura around its shape. He had watched silently as Billy's cries for help echoed along the riverbank, his heart pounding with each desperate plea.

The panic in Billy's eyes was etched in his memory, their gazes locking for a brief, agonizing moment. Pierce had wanted to act, to intervene, but the presence of Karl and Jake had held him back.

"Come on, Pierce. Let's go," Jake had said dismissively, yanking on Pierce's arm. "Let the pussy-boy figure it out for himself. Or maybe you like him. Do you like him, Pierce?"

"No, I don't like him one bit," Pierce had affirmed, his voice hollow.

The thought of Billy's dog, Finn, being swept away and lost forever brought a lump to his throat. Pierce had failed to act when it mattered most, a failure that haunted him in the suffocating quiet of his room.

His thoughts shifted to Jake and Karl. What if they had found out about his feelings for Billy when they were students together in high school? The verbal and physical assaults directed toward others who didn't conform to their narrow views still haunted him. He knew all too well the cruelty they were capable of. Pierce imagined his classmates' sneers and accusations, especially how they would react to what they saw as his disloyalty. He felt like Judas. He remembered how he'd shuddered at the thought of becoming their next target, of losing the fragile state of belonging he clung to.

But it wasn't just Billy who had suffered because of Pierce's fear and indecision. Friends and potential romantic interests had reached out to Pierce. He had turned them away, too afraid to let anyone see the real him. He could recall their pained expressions and confusion as they faced his cold rejection. Pierce had hurt people and left them feeling isolated and unworthy, all because he couldn't face his truth.

Then there was his father. Pierce knew all too well what his father thought about gay men and how he would respond whenever he encountered someone he perceived as queer. He could hear his father's stern voice proclaiming with disdain and disappointment, "Men don't act like that, Pierce. It's not normal." The cultural expectations of his Jamaican heritage weighed heavily on him. His father's strict views on masculinity and sexuality left no room for deviation. Pierce feared the look of disgust that would surely follow if his father learned the truth. The possibility of rejection, of being cast out, was a powerful deterrent.

His mother's reaction, however, was a bit harder to predict. She had always been more understanding, more compassionate. Pierce wondered if she would accept him for who he was or if she, too, would be swayed by his father's rigid beliefs. The uncertainty gnawed at him, adding another layer to his turmoil.

Pierce turned over, burying his face in his pillow, trying to silence the cacophony of thoughts. He imagined a world where he could be honest with Billy without hiding behind a facade of traditional masculinity. But that world felt so far away, an unattainable dream overshadowed by fear and familial pressure.

He regretted not helping Billy, not standing up to his friends, and not being true to himself. The guilt was a heavy burden, one that he carried alone. Pierce knew he couldn't go on like this forever, that something had to give. But for now, all he could do was hope for the strength to one day break free from the constraints that bound him, to find the courage to be himself, and to make amends for the moments he had erred.

Still haunted by the image of Billy's anguish, Pierce realized he needed to talk to someone who understood him and whom he could trust with his deepest regrets and fears. Marcus Sterling, his longtime friend and confidant since grade school, now working in finance on Wall Street, was the person he turned to in times like these. Pierce pulled out his phone, found Marcus's number in his contacts, and froze. If he were going to talk with Marcus about Billy and tell him how he felt, he'd also have to tell Marcus he was gay. He took a deep breath, exhaled slowly, and dialed.

"Hey, Marcus, can we talk? It's important," Pierce said, his voice tinged with desperation.

"Of course, man," Marcus replied. "What's going on?"

Pierce took another deep breath. "Do you remember Billy from high school? I need to get something off my chest about him and about me."

"Yeah, I remember Billy. What about him?"

Pierce hesitated before continuing. "There was a time when he needed help; it was back in high school, and I didn't do anything. I just stood there, scared of what Karl and Jake would think. But the truth is, I've always had feelings for Billy. I was just too afraid to admit it, even to myself."

"So, is this the part about you?"

"I'm gay, Marcus."

There was a pause on the other end of the line. Then Marcus's warm and steady voice came through. "Pierce, I'm happy you told me. Honestly, I was wondering when you'd figure it out. I've known for a while."

Pierce felt relieved and surprised. "You knew?"

"Yeah, man. It's something you can sense when you've been through it yourself. I'm gay too, Pierce."

Pierce was stunned. "You're gay? Why didn't you tell me?"

Marcus chuckled softly. "I figured you had enough on your plate. Plus, I wanted you to come to terms with your feelings in your own time. I'm here for you, Pierce, just like I always have been."

Pierce felt a wave of relief wash over him. "Thanks, Marcus. That means a lot."

"I want you to know that you're not alone in this. If you

ever need to talk, or if you're feeling down, call me. We'll get through this together, okay?"

Pierce's voice was thick with emotion. "I appreciate it, Marcus. Really."

"And about Billy," Marcus continued, "I know it's scary, but maybe it's time to tell him how you feel. You deserve to be happy, Pierce. You deserve to be with someone who makes you happy."

Pierce sighed. "You're right. I'll find the courage to be honest with him and myself. I promise I'll talk with him tomorrow after his shift." He ended the call.

His thoughts drifted to the encounter with Billy at La Péniche earlier that evening. Billy had placed a hand on Pierce's upper arm in a gesture of concern, and the sensations from their earlier embrace flared up inside him again.

Pierce Talon's behavior stemmed from a profound absence of common social emotions like shame and empathy. From a young age, he realized he didn't feel things like other kids did. He didn't experience guilt when he lied or compassion when classmates got hurt on the playground. Mostly, he felt nothing, and he despised the emptiness. So he sought ways to fill that void with…something.

His emotional skills lacked the finesse necessary for forming lasting friendships, often drifting between anxiety and apathy. Pierce believed his urge to act out was his brain's desperate attempt to replicate normalcy.

Complicating matters was his struggle with wanting to live as an openly gay man, particularly in the face of his father's homophobia. This added a layer of internal conflict, further fueling his erratic behavior. His father's lack of acceptance amplified the void he felt, intensifying his search for validation and belonging.

Pierce often made impulsive decisions, acting without considering the consequences. He also experienced frequent emotional outbursts, especially in stressful situations, adding to the instability in his relationships. He didn't see himself as a bad person or mentally unbalanced. Though his actions might not seem kind, he wasn't evil. He struggled with emotions and sought to fill the emptiness through his actions. Once he understood this about himself, he could control it better. This realization didn't make him a better person; it simply made him more effective at what he did.

Pierce channeled his need for sensation into his work as an executive chef. He impressed others with his culinary skills and sought excitement through manipulation and seduction. Stirring things up and deliberately flirting with couples to create tension and conflict entertained him and filled the void left by his father's rejection and his emotional emptiness.

As Pierce lay in bed, he replayed the concern he had seen on Billy's face and their conversation in his mind. He longed for a world where he could openly express his feelings, where helping Billy didn't come with the fear of judgment and rejection. The stream of thoughts flowed steadily, a constant amidst the uncertainties he faced. Pierce knew he would have to find his way, even if it meant navigating the treacherous waters of his fears and insecurities. It had been years since he had last seen Billy, but tonight's encounter had stirred emotions he hadn't felt for his former high school classmate in a long time.

Despite promising Marcus he would tell Billy how he felt, Pierce knew he wouldn't keep that promise—not yet, anyway. He wanted to, but he doubted he'd have the courage to do it tomorrow. Until then, he would hold onto the hope that love, like a river flowing to the sea, would find its way to him through whatever challenges lay ahead.

Billy arrived at the Sea Spray Inn's kitchen the following day, ready to help. Pierce greeted him with gratitude and nervousness.

"All right, Billy. Let's get you started. Have you ever worked in a kitchen before?" Pierce asked, trying to sound casual.

"Not professionally, but I can cook a mean breakfast," Billy replied.

Pierce chuckled. "Good, because that's where we're starting. I'll have a chef's jacket for you sometime this morning when the linen service restocks, but for now, grab an apron, and let's get to work."

As they moved around the kitchen, Pierce showed Billy how to use the industrial stove, the proper way to chop vegetables, and the secret to flipping pancakes without making a mess.

Billy fumbled with the spatula, sending a pancake flying. "Oops! Guess I need more practice."

Pierce laughed. "Don't worry, I've seen worse. You'll get the hang of it."

The two fell into an easy rhythm, the initial awkwardness giving way to friendly banter. Billy teased Pierce about his perfectionism, while Pierce couldn't help but laugh at Billy's clumsy but enthusiastic attempts.

By the end of the shift, the kitchen was bustling, and both men were exhausted but content. Pierce realized that working together might be the perfect way to bridge the gap between them and address his lingering feelings and regrets.

As they finished, the kitchen's hum quieted to a comfortable silence. Pierce glanced over at Billy, grateful for his presence but uncertain how to broach the subject gnawing at him.

"Hey, Billy, there's something I've been wanting to talk to you about," Pierce began, his voice faltering slightly. "Something from high school."

Billy looked at him with curiosity and concern. "What is it, Pierce?"

Pierce hesitated, the weight of the past bearing down on him. He thought about the years of unspoken guilt and the fear of rejection that had held him back. But standing here now, watching Billy's earnest face and feeling the easy camaraderie between them, he wasn't sure if now was the right time to revisit old wounds.

He took a deep breath and decided to leave the past where it was, at least for the moment. The present felt good, and he didn't want to ruin it. He smiled, shaking his head slightly. "Never mind, it can wait."

Billy looked puzzled but shrugged it off, smiling back. "All right, man. Whenever you're ready."

Pierce nodded. There would be a time to address the past, but he was content to let it rest now. They had made a start, and that was enough.

Chapter 4

Raindrops danced from the sky as sunlight pierced through the passing clouds. Thaddeus Quincy Lambert, III—Thad, to those who knew and worked with him—splashed through Lincoln Center Plaza's stunning collection of white travertine marble-clad theaters, concert halls, and its center-piece fountain. It was just after noon. He had plenty of time to catch the 1:42 train to Ocean Point. He'd walk instead of taking the subway to Penn Station; the rain was just a nuisance.

Once off the plaza, the city's black steel and concrete-gray buildings sparkled, their dark hues vibrant; even the dirt- and trash-filled gutters glistened as if wrapped in a glossy veneer. Nearly blinded by the dazzling display, he reached into his satchel—a well-worn gift from his parents for his eighteenth birthday. It was engraved with "TQL III" on a small brass nameplate, exuding refinement and elegance, designed to draw attention without being flashy or gaudy. He grabbed his cheap umbrella, the kind you bought on the street from pop-up opportunistic hawkers for a couple of bucks. Thad always bought the cheap ones, not trusting the integrity of the more expensive models or the vendor's lifetime guarantee. Who would you contact should your device malfunction? Customer service? Once the rain stopped, the peddler was nowhere to be found.

His flimsy device had a short lifespan, good for two storms at best; his had been through four and was currently suffering from three bent ribs and one missing altogether. He unfurled the umbrella; the canopy offered little protection from the rain. When he reached Columbus Circle, it turned inside out from a crosstown gust off the Hudson in the middle of an intersection. He tossed it into the closest trash receptacle.

He ducked in and out of doorways and under theater marquees from Broadway to Seventh Avenue, zigzagging through what remained of the sudden summer downburst toward Penn Station. At one point, with three blocks left to go before reaching the station, he heard a voice as it sliced through the deluge like a knife, scattering a choir of pigeons singing in the rain.

"Hey, you want a blow job?"

Thad skidded to a stop and turned towards the doorway from which the voice emanated. There, hiding from the rain, was a woman who looked like she'd just stepped off the stage of a burlesque show. No, wait, more like a cheap, glittered-out version of Botticelli's Venus working the skin trade. She was perched on a battered shell of what was once a cardboard box, its edges ripe for *papier-macheing*, her neon outfit an affront to subtlety.

"No thanks!" Thad replied.

She arched an overplucked eyebrow, and her sparkly eye shadow glowed through the rain-soaked air. "Aw, come on, honey."

Thad shook his head firmly, determined to make a clean escape. "Nope! I have to catch a train, and besides…"

But then, in a twist that could only happen in New York City, she dropped her voice a few octaves, transforming from

41

a neon-soaked siren to a down-to-earth confidante.

"Oh, I get it. I'm not your type, or are you into boys? That's OK, sweetie; enjoy your train ride. Hope whoever you're running off to see is as nice as you."

She darted back into her doorway haven, rain-thinned mascara running freely down her cheek, her progress punctuated by well-timed puddle jumps, blaming the rain for her current smeared condition. Thad chuckled as the sex worker tilted her head back, her arms raised and fists clenched, shouting her frustrations at an unseen god in an unforgiving heaven, "This is why we don't *do* outside!"

Thad quickened his pace toward Penn Station. He purchased his ticket, ran down the steps to the platform, and hopped aboard. He thought about what the street Venus had said about rushing off to be with someone. As far as he was concerned, his work came first. He had no time for dating or being in a relationship when he had a job and boss that demanded his full attention. He was single, maybe even happy when he thought about it, and he wanted to keep it that way.

Departing the platform, the train made its way through the labyrinth of underground tracks, each forming a complex network akin to a maze and each with its own destination. Once the train entered the tunnel under the Hudson River, he felt the air pressure build as the column of coaches, tightly connected like segments of a metallic centipede, undulated forward. Like multiple pairs of legs, the wheels worked in tandem, propelling the creature forward as it battled the trapped tunnel air. The air whooshed out of the tube just before the centipede's head emerged into the bright sunshine of New Jersey; the storm had passed.

A railroad crossing signal's flashing lights and lowered

gates caught his attention near Asbury Park. The pitch-altering Doppler effect of the signal's bell lingered in the air as the train chugged past.

Whispered conversations harmonized with the rhythmic pulse of the train as steel wheels percussed over rails. Now that he had left the chaos of his life back in the city, he took a deep breath. He was thirty years old and thriving. Ten years of hard work had paid off, though, and he now had the job of a lifetime: music director for a world-famous choreographer, Marsha Morgan, and her dance company. Marsha was beyond eccentric, but he discovered they worked well together. It was everything he had hoped for.

He drifted back to thoughts of being single. He was surrounded daily by available, beautiful people. Dancers. A few male dancers had even dared to ask him out on a date or to grab a quick cup of coffee after rehearsal. He never took them up on it, no matter how gorgeous they were or how much they insisted. He wasn't interested, and besides, how would his dating someone he worked with affect the well-being of the dance company? He didn't want to be accused of favoritism when it came time to cast roles for an upcoming performance. Yup, he was happy, single, and free.

The train from New York pulled into Ocean Point Depot, the last stop; Thaddeus Quincy Lambert, III, grabbed his well-worn brown leather satchel and a small, black portfolio and headed along the road to the Sea Spray Inn, just a short walk away.

Battleship gray-stained porch steps and salt-soaked siding gave the old structure a tired, weathered look that begged for a paint job. As he walked across the porch, sagging planks creaked, and stately columns shed chipped paint like dandruff.

A row of white rocking chairs was neatly arranged behind a white wooden railing supported by ornate lathed spindles. The view from the porch stretched across Ocean Boulevard to the beach and sea beyond.

He walked along the wrap-around veranda. A couple of elderly guests looked ghostlike, slumped in their rockers under the weight of white cotton blankets carefully tucked mummy-style around their frail bodies. They had either fallen asleep or died; it was hard to tell which. Nevertheless, they looked peaceful and worry-free, their faces familiar to Thad: the surviving relics of old wealthy New Jersey families like his own. Then, one of the cocoons twitched—a metamorphic miracle. This one's not dead. Eyes blinked through the noon-day sun and focused on Thad.

"Is that young Thad Lambert standing before me?"

Thad recognized the withered face poking out from her swaddled shroud. "Hello, Mrs. Winthrop. How are you doing today?"

Mrs. Winthrop was an old family friend who survived into her nineties. Despite her age, she never missed a thing and would tell you to your face what she thought about you or something you did, even when you didn't want to hear it.

"And your parents, dear? How are they doing? I miss them so."

"They're doing fine, Mrs. Winthrop, just fine. When I return to the city, I'll tell them you asked about them."

And with that, Mrs. Winthrop blinked twice, closed her eyes, and rejoined her dream already in progress.

When Thad was a boy, young families with children and their grandparents, including his, filled the Sea Spray Inn with inescapable joy and celebration. Most of his childhood contemporaries now opted for more exotic locations with modern accommodations, fancy restaurants, and upscale entertainment, while others owned shore homes secured safely behind gated driveways. But not Thad. He continued to visit each summer for at least a week or two. Some of that had to do with tradition, and some of it was to find inspiration for his work, the old hotel being a haven for his creativity. Unfortunately, his parents no longer made an effort to spend time here. They were older and preferred the luxury of their Upper East Side apartment or the occasional holiday in France. Or maybe it was just too sad for them to return to this place where each passing year reminded them of longtime friends and loved ones no longer with them.

It felt different today, a melancholy of spent lives, unfulfilled dreams, and missed loved ones. The hotel's surviving guests had dwindled to a handful of widowed wives, an assortment of spinster aunts, and the occasional aging bachelor uncle, all struggling to keep up appearances and hold onto traditions in a place built just for them. Their time was running out. Thad might have found the old inn too depressing if he wasn't on vacation. But here he was, and it was his family's tradition, too, even if he was the only one still making the yearly journey there.

Thad walked into the lobby, which also served as the hotel's common room and lounge. The grandeur of the space was undeniable, a nostalgic echo of a bygone era. It looked the same as it had when he was a child, when his father was a child, and when his grandfather was a child. The lobby was a study in faded opulence, with potted palms strategically placed to draw the eye away from the long-faded wallpaper that hinted at once vibrant patterns now muted with age. The walls, adorned with gold-framed paintings of seascapes and pastoral scenes, added a touch of faded elegance.

Newspapers, looking as if they'd been freshly ironed, were draped on bamboo rods and racked for easy access, their crisp rustling a faint background to the room's quiet conversations. In the lobby, wicker furniture with tropical floral print cushions provided a semblance of comfort. These were the places where guests could sit and reminisce over glasses of port after dinner, the cushions sagging with the weight of countless conversations. The smell of old books and musty upholstery mingled with the salt from the sea, creating a scent that was as much a part of the hotel as its creaky floorboards.

Large bay windows, framed by heavy, draped curtains, filtered the sunlight entering the room, producing a gentle luminosity that danced on the polished wooden floors. The light highlighted the dust particles floating in the air, a drifting tapestry of sand from the beach, salt from the sea, and specks of dead skin moving idly in the summer heat. These windows offered a glimpse of the ocean beyond, a constant reminder of the world outside, yet somehow feeling like a distant memory.

Dominating the center of the room was a massive wooden staircase, its banisters carved with intricate details of seashells and waves, leading to the three upper floors. The creak of each step was a testament to the countless feet that had trodden up and down over the decades. The staircase's central location meant that any movement, any conversation on the upper floors cascaded down into the lobby, keeping the guests connected to the pulse of the hotel.

To the left of the lobby, through an ample, arched doorway flanked by marble columns, lay the common room, doubling as a lounge area. Unlike the airy wicker furniture in the lobby, this space was filled with overstuffed armchairs and vintage chaise lounges upholstered in rich, velvety fabrics that had long since lost their original luster. A grand piano sat in one corner, its top strewn with sheet music and a faded photograph of a long-forgotten pianist. The soft melodies played by a visiting musician or an adventurous guest would drift through the archway, filling the lobby with a gentle, nostalgic air. A large fireplace dominated one wall, its mantel decorated with an assortment of porcelain figurines and dusty trinkets that had seen better days. During storms or on cooler evenings, the crackle of a wood-burning fire served as the backdrop to whispered conversations and the clinking of teacups.

Directly across from the lounge, accessible through another archway, was the dining room. Despite its grandeur, this space felt somewhat constrained; every table and chair was meticulously arranged as if to maximize the visibility of the room's occupants. The high ceilings were adorned with elaborate crystal chandeliers, their glass prisms casting rainbows of light across the room during the day and an inviting glow at night. Polished tables—long, short, square, and round—set with fine china, silverware, and a solitary vase cradling a vibrant yellow rose in a translucent glow filled the room, each nodding to a time when formal dining was the norm. Thad couldn't recall roses in previous years. Typically, the tables boasted modest arrangements of wildflowers plucked from the borders surrounding the front veranda and the untamed patches behind the hotel. But he liked how the roses added an understated elegance to the room.

From any corner of the dining room, one could overhear the murmur of conversations from the lounge, the soft rustling of newspapers from the lobby, and even the gentle plink of piano keys. The proximity of these spaces ensured that no conversation remained entirely private, each word, each laugh, subtly shared among the guests. The dining room's large windows mirrored those in the lobby, offering an ocean view that provided a backdrop of tranquility, complementing the room's hushed chatter and the quiet clinking of cutlery.

As Thad stood in the lobby, he could see the guests drifting between the array of rooms, their subdued chitchat and gentle movements starkly contrasting the vibrant life the hotel once knew. The interconnectedness of these spaces meant that Thad could feel the pulse of the entire hotel from his spot, a place where memories lingered and the past seemed perpetually present. It was a place where lives were intertwined, secrets were shared in whispers, dreams still attainable were quietly nurtured, and those lost to time were abandoned.

Thad's cologne, activated by his walk to the hotel, released a spicy blend of cardamom, cinnamon, and nutmeg, combined with aromatic juniper and cedarwood, reminiscent of a summer forest. This sophisticated scent mingled with the old structure's aroma: a shuttered mustiness and old polished wood, faint floral notes, an earthiness from the potted palms, hints of ink and paper, and brined air, evoking the nostalgia of grand old hotels and the allure of coastal retreats.

But the magic in the room, for Thad especially, was the grand piano silently waiting for him between the staircase and sitting area. It was the same piano that Thad had played as a small child to an enthusiastic audience of guests and staff almost every evening. It's where his parents discovered that he was talented, even though Thad had been taking lessons at home since he was three. It was where his dreams of becoming a musician began, and his future took shape. It was also where, years later, when he was twenty and a student at Juilliard, he composed his first significant ballet opus. That's when the New York City dance world took notice of his talent. Now he was thirty, and even though he preferred his current role as music director and conductor and did little, if any, composing anymore, he had made a name for himself thanks in part, he mused, to that piano.

He approached the front desk and rang the bell. He noticed a group of hotel workers: a staff meeting in progress in the adjoining dining room. A few of the staff looked familiar from previous seasons. He remembered Sarah, a poised and experienced waitress who had spent several summers working at the hotel. Her calm demeanor and quick thinking made her a natural leader among less experienced servers. Two other twenty-somethings sat beside her. They were most likely college students on summer break needing to make some cash before the fall semester. He could guess their roles by how they were dressed: servers who doubled as housekeepers, a handyman, and a chef he'd recognized from last season. They were seated at a large, round oak table.

Waiting for someone to check him in, he heard Sarah raise a concern. "A very shaky shelf holds stacks of plates over the cooktop. It needs to be fixed right away. It's precarious."

"Duly noted, Sarah," the chef responded. "Consider it taken care of." He made eye contact with another young man at the table. "I have just the person to do it."

The chef introduced the young man, handing him a chef's jacket, hat, and name tag. The man stood, tried on the coat, pulled his shaggy hair back, secured it with a stretchy hair tie, and then donned his cap. The workers applauded his transformation. The new guy was cute, too, Thad thought.

The hotel manager, Ronald Service, sat just outside the circle. He spotted Thad at the front desk and excused himself from the meeting.

"Mr. Lambert, so good to see you again. Welcome back to the Sea Spray Inn. We have your suite ready. If you sign the register, I'll get your key and someone to carry your luggage."

"I've got it, Ron. I'm traveling light this year, only this satchel and a few manuscripts." He pointed to his bag and portfolio.

The manager turned to the guest mailboxes behind the front desk, grabbed an old brass skeleton key, and placed it on the counter. The engraved oval tag read 3A, the same third-floor suite that Thad had rented for as long as he had been coming to the inn alone. It had the best views and cooling sea breezes at night.

"Oh, and we have a new chef, Pierce Talon; he's the one in the hat." Ron gestured toward the group around the table. "He worked here last summer and just graduated from a culinary institute in the city. Can you imagine being a chef at that young age? The guests are raving about his menu."

"I remember Pierce. He held a lot of promise as a rising culinary star. I look forward to enjoying his cuisine while I'm here." Thad had had little interaction with Pierce the previous summer, but he recalled how he came off with a distinct cockiness, an air of confidence that was evident in his swagger.

"And, if I could be so forward and if you're so moved, I hope you will regale us with a few tunes on the piano some night. The guests would be so appreciative if you did."

Thad smiled. "I'm sure that can be arranged, Ron."

Thad picked up his key, grabbed his bag and portfolio, and headed toward the staircase. He glanced over toward the dining room. Everyone had left the meeting except for one, the man who received the new chef's jacket, hat, and name tag. He was making a list on a small, wire-bound notebook. Thad noticed the man's light brown hair streaked by the summer sun. He saw the curve of his tan neck and broad shoulders. He thought his hands were beautiful, strong yet graceful, the type that should be playing the piano.

The young man pushed back his chair with a clatter, hastily tucking his notepad into the breast pocket of his new chef's jacket. He shot up, ready to dart back into the bustling chaos of the kitchen. But his trajectory was off as he collided head-on with Thad at the foot of the staircase. The impact dislodged Thad's portfolio case, sending a cascade of music manuscript pages across the hardwood floor.

"Hey, watch it!"

His accent carried a unique intonation pattern and rhythm: a rapid pace with a certain energy and enthusiasm, the matter-of-fact brusqueness of a young man from New Jersey. Instinctively, he grabbed Thad's arms to steady himself, his eyes locking with Thad's for a moment before offering a crooked grin as his defensive edge softened.

"Sorry about that."

Thad arched an eyebrow. "Do you mind letting go now?"

The young man looked down, almost surprised to find his hands holding onto Thad's arms. A flush crept up his neck, coloring his cheeks as he hastily withdrew his hands. Then he went to his knees and began collecting the scattered sheaf of papers covering the floor. Thad noticed how the young man took the time to place the sheets back in order and realized that he could read music.

"What's all this?"

"It's music. I'm a musician, and this…" Thad gestured to the stack of pages the man held, "is what I do."

"You compose?"

"No, not really. I'm a music director, and this is material I'm preparing for the fall."

"Sorry, I made a mess of it." He returned the bundle to Thad, who placed it in the portfolio. "I'm in music, too. A music teacher at the local elementary school. I'm off for the summer." A huge smile took over his face.

Thad nodded and thought, that's interesting; what's this guy doing in a place like this? He noted the name tag on the man's jacket: *Billy*.

There was a moment of silent discomfort, both men standing and looking at the other. The young man said, "Please…" gesturing for Thad to continue his climb up to his room.

"No, I insist. You're in a hurry, and I'm not, so you go ahead. Billy, is it?"

"No, please. You first. You're a guest here, after all."

"Well, thanks, Billy. I appreciate it," Thad replied before climbing the stairs. Billy turned abruptly and disappeared around the corner and out of sight.

Thad climbed the three flights of stairs to his room. He jiggled the key in the lock, opened the door, and dropped his bag and portfolio on the floor. He crossed to the window and lifted the sash. The breeze caught the lace curtains and sent them fluttering into the room. He looked east across Ocean Boulevard and out to the ocean beyond. He loved this place where the sea, sand, and sky met.

Thad unfastened his neatly packed satchel, reflecting on his life in New York and demanding career. His West Village apartment, a testament to his disciplined nature, came to mind—everything meticulously in its place. As he carefully placed his perfectly pressed and folded clothes in the dresser, his thoughts drifted to the pivotal moments that defined his career, especially his complex relationship with his boss and mentor, Marsha Morgan.

Thad's journey in music had been rigorous, marked by both highs and lows. He recalled the pressure Marsha had placed on him, her high expectations driving him to excel. As he settled into his room, preparing for a much-needed retreat, he hoped the break would bring peace and productivity—a chance to reflect on his path and contemplate where it might lead him.

He was free for the next two weeks. He'd work on the program for the dance company's late fall season to determine the number of musicians he'd need for the orchestra and small ensembles but was in no rush. He knew most of the material by heart, all the pieces for the upcoming season he had conducted before, with one exception. He'd commissioned a new piece by Emile Beauvais for the company's principal dancer, Liam Mercer. And while he hadn't heard from the composer since the commission was offered, Thad knew Emile was reliable and would deliver it on time. Even so, he was beginning to wonder why he hadn't received it yet, and he didn't want that *wonder* to become worry.

And he'd offer the guests an evening of music and song, not just because Ron had asked but because it was expected. Still, Thad promised himself he'd relax and recharge while he was here, and then he chuckled to himself, remembering the brusque encounter with the young man with the beautiful hands in the lobby, how he grabbed Thad with those hands when they collided by the stairs. Billy, was it?

Chapter 5

When Billy entered the kitchen, Sarah was talking with Emily and Nathan, two enthusiastic college students working for the season, eager to gain hospitality industry experience. He pulled out his notepad and flipped through the pages to ensure he had jotted down their names. Names were important to Billy. He was about to join their conversation when he noticed Pierce scowling at him from across the room.

"Where have you been, Billy?" Pierce's voice carried through the cozy confines of the Sea Spray Inn's kitchen, laced with curiosity and a hint of concern that felt more like a demand.

"Oh…Hi, Pierce." Billy's face lit up as he approached the back, where Pierce sat at a butcher block prep table, finalizing the evening menu. Billy peeled off his brand-new chef's coat and hung it on one of the pegs by the door. The pristine white coat contrasted sharply with the organized chaos of the kitchen.

"What happened to you? The meeting ended a while ago," Pierce inquired, his brows knitting together as he approached Billy. The usual spark in his eyes was replaced with something darker, more intense.

"I was just going over my notes from the meeting, and on my way back to the kitchen, I accidentally bumped into one of the guests. I don't know his name, but he was nice about the whole thing," Billy replied, his voice tinged with embarrassment. He could feel the weight of Pierce's gaze, a feeling that made him uncomfortable.

"I hoped you'd come right back to the kitchen. I wanted to go over a couple of things in private with you," Pierce said, his tone severe. Billy sensed an edge in Pierce's voice, hinting at something he couldn't quite place—was it jealousy or something else?

"It was an accident." Billy shook free from Pierce's grasp. "I didn't mean to crash into him." Billy's tone was defensive. He wasn't accustomed to not talking to patrons, especially as a piano player who made sure he connected with his customers at La Péniche.

"Stick to the kitchen during your shift, Billy. It's better that way," Pierce advised, his tone softening as he placed a reassuring hand on Billy's shoulder. His touch lingered a moment too long. Billy felt fenced in.

"Aye, aye, captain," Billy replied with a grin, his usual cheerful demeanor returning. He decided to brush off the uneasy feeling, though the intensity of Pierce's concern still gnawed at him.

Pierce glanced at the unstable shelf above the cooktop and then back at Billy. "By the way, don't forget to fix the loose shelf over the cooktop. The tools are in the storage room next to the pantry. I'll show you where they are." Pierce stood, and Billy followed him to the storage room, where Pierce pointed out a toolbox on a lower shelf. "Here you go. Should be everything you need," Pierce said, handing it to Billy. "If you need anything else, there's a workshop in the bunkhouse behind the hotel with wood scraps and hardware for routine repairs."

Billy watched Pierce's smile return as he slipped back into his chair at the prep table and resumed working on the menu. "Okay, then. I'll see you tomorrow morning. You did a great job today; maybe I'll sleep in and catch up with you after the breakfast service. Do you think you can handle it on your own?"

"I do, Pierce, but I thought you wanted to discuss something. You said 'privately,'" Billy reminded him.

"Yeah, I do. Maybe another time. Don't you have to get ready for your gig at La Péniche tonight?" Pierce inquired. The casual tone of his words didn't mask the tension in his gaze, as if he were holding back something significant.

"We can put it off until later if you want, but I've got a little time right now."

"Okay, then. Here's the deal: I need this kitchen to run smoothly this summer. I can't afford any screw-ups."

"What do you mean?"

"Well, I've got this great job lined up for later in the fall in New York. I don't want anything to go wrong here that could impact securing that job. Chefs tend to hang out with chefs. They all talk to each other like it's a special club. And I don't want them talking about me if something goes wrong here. I already had one cook walk out on me."

"It'll be okay, Pierce. You seem to know what you're doing, and from what I've seen today, the kitchen runs smoothly."

"Thanks, Billy. Just keep an eye on things, okay?"

"Will do," Billy nodded, taking the toolbox and heading to the cooktop. He examined the loose shelf, noticing it was wobbling precariously. It needed more than just tightening the screws.

First, Billy carefully removed the plates and other items

from the shelf, setting them aside on the nearby counter to avoid accidents. He unscrewed the shelf from the wall, carefully lifting it away and placing it on the floor.

With the shelf removed, Billy inspected the old screw holes. They'd become compromised, enlarged, preventing the screws from gripping properly. He used a handheld vacuum from the storage room to clean out the old screw holes, removing any debris and dust that had accumulated over time.

Looking through the toolbox, Billy found a tube of quick-setting wood adhesive but no dowels or filler. He ran out to the workshop and found some wood scraps he could use. Using a coping saw from the toolbox, he cut the scraps into thin strips that could fit into the screw holes.

Billy injected a small amount of adhesive into each of the old screw holes. He then inserted the wooden strips into the holes, trimming any excess to ensure they were flush with the wall surface. He let the adhesive and wooden strips set for a few minutes, creating an improved base for the screws to be reinserted.

While waiting, Billy examined the shelf itself. Noticing some of the screw holes on the shelf were also a bit worn, he used the same method with the wood adhesive and wooden scraps to fill those holes. Once the adhesive had dried, he removed the rough edges using sandpaper from the toolbox and redrilled new pilot holes.

He examined the old screws and discarded them. He rummaged through the toolbox and found a small box of assorted screws. He picked the ones that matched the needed size and set them aside.

After the adhesive and wooden strips had fully set, Billy repositioned the shelf against the wall, aligning it carefully.

Holding the shelf in place, Billy began screwing it back onto the wall. He double-checked the shelf's stability, gently pushing and pulling it to ensure it was firmly in place.

Satisfied with the result, Billy placed the plates and items back onto the shelf, arranging them neatly.

"There, all done," Billy said, admiring his work.

Clutching his notebook tightly, Billy exited down the back steps to where his bike lay chained, an uneasy awareness prickling at the back of his neck. He sensed Pierce's eyes shadowing him with an intensity that seemed to bore into his back. As Billy fumbled with the chain at the bottom of the stair rail, a swift glance revealed Pierce retreating, his gaze sliding away in a guilty slither, vanishing behind the kitchen door with a haste that left the air charged with a silent, unsettling question. The possessiveness in Pierce's eyes lingered in Billy's mind, leaving him wondering what Pierce feared.

Chapter 6

Thad stepped onto the porch of the Inn, smiling as he took in the rhythmic crash of the waves and the seagulls' laughing cries. A saltwater mist enveloped families strolling back from the beach. The line of sun-kissed, tousled-hair families reminded Thad of a safari, with porters hauling the day's necessities. Some pulled wagons filled with beach toys, pails, and tiny shovels for castle construction, while others balanced ice chests on their heads. Children dragged colorful, striped towels through the sand and along the sidewalk, returning to their camp for the night. Laughter and snippets of conversation floated up to him, a joyful cacophony of children recounting their adventures and discoveries.

Across the street, stately summer homes and quaint cottages stood in defiance of the setting sun, their west-facing walls and windows aglow with the day's last light. Shadows stretched long across manicured lawns and gardens, with light filtering through the leaves of oak and maple trees, casting intricate patterns on the ground. The eastern facades of these houses were painted in delicate, pastel hues, creating a beautiful contrast against the blue ocean behind them.

Inside the Sea Spray Inn, Thad entered the dining room. The place buzzed with guests, and the aroma of freshly prepared seafood wafted through the kitchen's propped-open door. And there, amidst the organized chaos of the kitchen, was Pierce Talon, who commanded the bustle like a maestro leading an orchestra. His sharp wit and magnetic charm were on full display as he led his team with precision, occasionally flashing a seductive grin that could melt hearts and ice cream.

Thad paused by the open kitchen door, watching Pierce with fascination and amusement. He recalled an incident from a year ago during a previous stay at the hotel when Pierce, then the chef's apprentice, had attempted to stage a coup against his mentor. The event became the talk of the hotel, mainly due to the chef's highly temperamental reaction, which included wailing, weeping, and threats of expelling Pierce from his summer practicum and reporting his mischievous tendencies to the culinary school. Despite the drama, Thad was intrigued by Pierce. He couldn't deny his attraction to the chef, but he sensed darker instincts beneath that allure—a feeling that Pierce's charm could swiftly turn into a weapon.

Their paths had crossed several times at the Sea Spray Inn the previous year, but this year felt different. Perhaps it was the magic of being at the shore or Pierce's magnetic charm at work. Or maybe Pierce was no more than a predatory flirter. Thad grappled with these conflicting feelings—the irresistible attraction and the nagging apprehension. He was drawn to Pierce's confidence, yet something about his behavior sent a warning signal, a cautionary whisper that perhaps Pierce's charisma masked something more insidious.

Their eyes met briefly as Pierce stepped out of the kitchen, carrying a plate of garlicky mussels on a bed of expertly prepared al dente linguine. Thad felt a surge of heat spread through him, captivated by the chef's presence. At that moment, Thad trusted his gut's reaction to Pierce. Instead of sitting down for a meal, he headed to the lobby lounge for safety's sake, opting for distance over potential entanglement.

In the lounge, his thoughts lingered on Pierce and the chaotic energy of the kitchen. He sat at the grand piano, letting his fingers glide over the keys, producing a soft, contemplative melody that echoed his internal turmoil—a bittersweet harmony resonating with his conflicted feelings.

The lounge was quiet, with only a few guests sipping their evening drinks. As Thad played, he was drawn into the haunting strains of "The Anniversary Waltz," a ballad from the Forties based on an old Romanian tune. Though he never considered himself a contemporary pianist—he preferred the classics—the music flowed effortlessly from his fingers, each note reflecting his inner struggle. His mind wandered back to the young chef, Billy, whose unexpected impact on him was still palpable. During their first meeting by the stairs, Billy's firm grip had left a literal bruise on Thad's arm and an indelible mark on his emotions. The memory of that seemingly innocuous yet lingering touch troubled him in ways he couldn't quite understand. The unexpected warmth of Billy's hand, the unspoken intensity of his grip, and the fleeting yet palpable connection stirred something deep within Thad—a curiosity and disorientation he found difficult to shake.

An elderly couple approached as he played, their faces lighting up with recognition. The woman's eyes sparkled with a gentle light, and she leaned on her husband's arm for support.

"Excuse us," she said softly, nostalgia lacing her voice. "But that piece you're playing...it's a song we dance to every year on our wedding anniversary, more than fifty years ago. You're playing it beautifully."

Thad paused, smiling at the couple. "Thank you. It's a

beautiful piece, isn't it? One of my favorites."

The man nodded appreciatively, his eyes misting with memories. "It's lovely. We hope to hear you play more during our stay. It brings back so many cherished memories."

Thad felt a deep bond with the couple, their enduring love a poignant contrast to his own tangled emotions. "I'd be honored to play for you both. Music has a way of bringing back the best parts of our past, doesn't it?"

"Yes, it does," the woman replied, her voice soft with emotion. "Thank you for sharing it with us. It means more than you know."

Thad thanked them and resumed playing as the couple turned towards each other and waltzed back to where they had been seated.

Ron Service approached Thad with a smile as the evening sun dipped toward the horizon. "Thad, could you play a few more tunes for the guests? They've been loving your music."

"Of course, Ron," Thad replied, his fingers moving to a familiar melody. As he played, the lounge gradually filled with guests, drawn by the enchanting music.

Satisfied with his decision to avoid the dining room and avert a potentially complicated situation with Pierce, he could focus on what he truly loved—bringing joy to others through his music. As melodies flowed from his fingers, Thad was reminded that sometimes stepping back is the best way to move forward.

Chapter 7

Thad sat at the small writing desk and looked out the opened window to the sea. The gentle sea breeze ruffled the curtains as he stared at the stack of music slated for the dance company's December season. The rhythmic sound of waves crashing against the shore usually brought him solace, a wellspring of creative energy. Yet today, despite the idyllic setting, his thoughts were scattered, his mind restless.

He drummed his fingers on the desk, fixated on the blank space in the program for Emile Beauvais's unfinished composition. It was meant to be the season's highlight, the piece that would weave the entire program into a seamless tapestry. Without it, everything felt disjointed, lacking the harmony he sought.

Emile's recent messages were filled with excuses: creative blocks, personal issues, and technical problems with his composing software. "I'm a perfectionist," he wrote. "Nothing I create feels good enough to finalize. I need more time." Thad understood the pressures of perfectionism, but the delay was becoming a critical flaw in his carefully crafted plan.

The weight of the missing piece pressed down on him. It was time for a break, he thought. A walk and eating something could be the distraction he needed to clear his mind.

Descending the staircase, he made his way to the kitchen.

Peeking inside, he saw Billy kneading dough with focused determination. The sight was mesmerizing—the graceful rhythm of his movements, the simplicity and focus he brought to his work. It reminded Thad of the creative process, whether in the kitchen or on stage, requiring patience and passion.

Thad cleared his throat, not wanting to startle the young chef. Billy turned, flour dusting his hands and apron, and smiled when he saw Thad. "Oh, it's you again," he said, wiping his hands on a towel. "Sorry about our collision yesterday."

Thad smiled back. "No need to apologize. I was curious to see what you were cooking."

Billy's face lit up with a grin. "Just helping Pierce with some bread. He had to run a few errands. Did you eat lunch? We still have some seafood chowder on the stove if you want to try it."

"I'd love to," Thad replied. As Billy ladled a steaming bowl of chowder, Thad felt immediately at ease. Holding both bowls and a couple of soup spoons, Billy gestured toward a small table in the corner of the kitchen, the aroma of the chowder adding to the intimate, cozy atmosphere. Thad joined him at the table and continued, "You could tell me about your culinary journey. You told me you taught music, but how did you become a chef at this hotel?"

Billy did a double-take as he passed the bowl to Thad. "I'm no chef! I'm just helping out an old classmate, Pierce. He's the Wonder Boy chef. This is his chowder."

Their conversation continued between spoonfuls of chowder, and Thad was drawn to Billy's candid and unpretentious manner.

"If you don't mind me asking, you said you were a music director. What exactly does that entail?" Billy's curiosity seemed genuine, and Thad appreciated the opportunity to share his passion.

Thad told Billy about his career as a music director and his work with the Marsha Morgan Dance Company. He spoke of the challenges of creating a cohesive program, the joy of seeing a piece come to life on stage, and the constant pursuit of perfection. Billy listened intently, his eyes reflecting a deep respect and admiration. When Thad finished giving Billy a glimpse into his work, he asked Billy about his teaching.

"So, tell me about your school and your music program."

"I teach kids basic music fundamentals, a little theory, music appreciation, and I have a chorus for anyone interested in singing, but it's nothing as important as the work that you're doing."

"Don't underestimate the importance of your work. We need people like you to teach children music so they can grow up and follow their dreams like I'm doing today. It's noble work, Billy." Thad's words were sincere, and he felt a bond forming between them, a closeness forged by their shared love of music.

Thad returned to his suite with a newfound purpose. Billy's humility around his teaching seemed to rub off on Thad, and his notes on the project looked needlessly complicated. He disregarded them now, and with a vision of Billy's handsome smile in his mind, he effortlessly rearranged the program, leaving a spot open for Emile's piece in the second half of the program immediately preceding the final number. There was still work to be done, but the program had balance now, and Thad felt confident that Marsha would approve his selections. It was as if the meeting with Billy had unlocked a door to his creativity, reigniting the spark he had been missing.

Chapter 8

The next morning, Thad awoke early, eager to start his day. He had spent a second restless night thinking about his chance encounter with Billy. The young music teacher had left a lasting impression on him, and Thad couldn't wait to see him again.

He dressed quickly and headed downstairs to the dining room for breakfast. The Sea Spray Inn was known for its delicious morning meals, and Thad was excited to try the spread. As he entered the dining room, he noticed Billy and a few servers busy at work, arranging plates and silverware on the tables.

"Good morning, Billy," Thad greeted him enthusiastically.

Billy looked up, surprised to see Thad there so early. "Oh, good morning, Mr. Lambert. I didn't expect to see you down here so soon."

"Please, call me Thad," he insisted. "Whatever you're cooking smells delicious. It's been a while since I've had a hearty seaside breakfast."

Billy grinned. "Well, you're in for a treat."

Thad sat at a table by the window, and Billy brought over a menu. As Thad perused the options, he found himself stealing glances at Billy. The morning light kissed his features, making him even more captivating.

When Thad finally made his selection, choosing a stack of blueberry pancakes with a side of bacon, he asked Billy, "So, you told me how you got here cooking at the inn, but how do you like it?"

Billy leaned against a nearby chair, his eyes sparkling with enthusiasm. "It's an experience, that's for sure. The guests are lovely, and the inn has a rich history. Plus, it's allowed me to make some extra dollars this summer."

Thad nodded in agreement. "It's a special place filled with memories. I fondly remember playing the grand piano in the lounge as a child."

Billy's eyes lit up. "You play the piano? That's incredible! You should play for the guests one evening. I'm sure they'd love it. I'll talk to Ron Service about it."

Thad smiled. "That's okay, Billy. Ron asked if I'd play when I checked in. And I did last night for a bit."

Their conversation flowed effortlessly, and Thad felt a magnetic pull between them, a familiarity he couldn't ignore. As they chatted about music and shared memories of Beachside and Ocean Point, Thad hoped that this summer at the Sea Spray Inn would be one to remember.

A few more guests arrived, and Billy had to return to the kitchen as the breakfast rush began picking up. Thad reluctantly finished his meal, spearing the last bit of syrupy pancake, and bid farewell to Billy, promising to meet again later in the day. He left the dining room, eager to see where this unexpected encounter with the charming music teacher would lead.

Chapter 9

Billy sat at the grand piano in the elegant lounge of the Sea Spray Inn. Lunch had ended, and the guests had dispersed for their afternoon activities. Some took naps, others relaxed on the front porch, and a few ventured out for a stroll along the beach. Billy, however, had the luxury of free time and intended to make the most of it; his shift was over, and La Péniche was closed on Mondays, so his time was his for the rest of the day.

His fingers intertwined, he stretched out his arms, palms facing outward, feeling the pleasant tension in his muscles. He released the stretch and pressed one hand against the knuckles of the other until he felt a satisfying pop. He did the same with the other hand, relishing the enjoyable release. After shaking out both hands, he turned to the grand piano before him.

Today, he had something special in mind. It was a new composition, a piece he was working on, and he was eager to play through what he had written without interruption. He wanted to ensure that the music he now played in real-time was consistent with the haunting melody he had harbored for years, waiting for it to blossom fully, a melody to give his grief a name, a tonal therapy meant to purge his sadness about the loss of Finn. He knew that creative ideas, especially a new musical composition, could take time to mature before they fit together as a completed piece.

As he settled onto the piano bench, his eyes were drawn to a vase of yellow roses on a nearby table. Seeing the roses, even just a single stem, comforted Billy. They were his mother's favorite and grew beautifully in her summer garden, reminding Billy of his childhood and happier times. He had also noticed the same cheerful yellow roses adorning the dining room earlier, and he appreciated the thoughtful design motif as if someone had carried over the theme from one space in the hotel to another, creating a seamless flow throughout the inn.

His fingers gently caressed the keys, coaxing the grand piano to life with a soft, melodic prelude. As he played, he reflected on his deepening fondness for Thad. Thad's gentleness contrasted sharply with the more forceful personalities Billy was used to, especially Pierce. Thad's interest in him was untainted by the competition and jealousy that often clouded his interactions with others, particularly a few musicians who felt threatened by Billy's talent. Could this be something more, something that went beyond the fleeting infatuations and superficial flirtations he'd encountered before?

Yet, there was also a part of him that was wary. His past experiences taught him to be cautious and guard his heart against the pain of unfulfilled promises and broken dreams. Pierce's possessiveness had been a constant reminder of the dangers of letting someone get too close. But Thad was different. His interest seemed to stem from genuine curiosity and kindness, not the controlling intensity that Pierce often displayed.

"You said you taught music, but I didn't know you played the piano. Not like that."

Billy's hands fell to his thighs, and he turned to see who had interrupted his playing. When he saw Mr. Lambert standing beside him, his face lit up with surprise and delight.

"Mr. Lambert," he began, then corrected himself with an embarrassed grin. "Thad, where did you come from? I thought I was alone."

Thad Lambert was a man of grace and charm. His sandy blond hair framed a handsome face, and his eyes held a tender expression that was hard to resist. He was a favorite among the staff and guests, and his presence brightened even the cloudiest days.

Thad grinned, his eyes twinkling with amusement. "I'm sorry to interrupt, but whatever you're playing is beautiful. What is it?"

Billy turned back to the piano, a faint blush coloring his cheeks. "It's a piece I'm working on. I haven't given it a name yet, but I wanted to hear how it sounded outside my head."

Thad took a step closer, his curiosity piqued. "May I listen?"

Billy nodded, his fingers returning to the keys. As the first notes of his composition filled the room, a wave of vulnerability washed over him. He rarely played his pieces for anyone, and no one ever asked him to, but something about Thad's presence made it feel right.

As he played, Billy's mind wandered. He was struck by how natural it felt to share this part of himself with Thad. The vulnerability of exposing his unfinished work felt less like a risk and more like an opportunity. He wondered if Thad felt the same, if he sensed the unspoken words and emotions Billy poured into each note.

The music swirled around them, telling a story of loss. Billy's fingers moved effortlessly across the keys, each note a testament to his passion for music and life and the sadness beneath the melody's surface.

Billy thought about Finn, the friend he'd lost, and the sorrow that had never entirely faded. The music became a conduit for his grief, expressing the pain that words could never capture. As he played, he felt the weight of his emotions lift slightly, replaced by calm and clarity.

As the song's final chord faded into the room's quiet, Billy noticed Thad had closed his eyes, seemingly surrendering to the music. Watching him, Billy felt almost like an intruder into this private reverie. When the last echo died away, a serene calm settled over them. Thad's eyes opened, his smile appreciative, as if the two men had shared something profound. As Billy waited for Thad to speak about the piece he'd just played, he became acutely aware of Thad's cologne—a spicy hint of cinnamon mingled with a woodsy essence, like being in a forest.

"That's as far as I've gotten with it."

"That was beautiful, Billy. You have a remarkable talent."

Billy stood up; his heart swelled with pride and gratitude. "Thank you, Mr. Lambert. It means a lot coming from you."

Thad stepped closer until he stood beside Billy, their shoulders touching. "I meant what I said before, you know," he whispered. "Call me Thad. And if you ever want to play that beautiful piece again, I'll be here to listen."

Their eyes locked, and in that moment, the world outside the Sea Spray Inn ceased to exist. Billy's heart raced, and he realized that this chance encounter with Thad might be the beginning of something truly magical.

As he looked into Thad's eyes, Billy felt a gentle heat radiate within him, a sensation he hadn't felt in a long time. There was something here, something more profound than mere attraction. It was as if Thad saw him for who he truly was beyond the walls he had built around his heart. This realization made Billy wonder if he could trust Thad and let someone into his life in a way he hadn't dared for years.

In the fading afternoon light filtering through the windows and enveloping the piano and the two men by its side, Billy sensed the Sea Spray Inn's unique talent for intertwining lives and tales into its rich tapestry of history. As the soft strains of their unspoken bond lingered in the air, Billy couldn't wait to see where this new chapter would lead.

Billy noticed Pierce observing them from the dining room doorway, half-hidden but unmistakably present. He sensed Pierce's growing unease. It was clear to Billy that Pierce felt something more than just music was brewing between the two men, even if Billy and Thad hadn't fully realized it.

Unable to bear the situation any longer, Pierce decided to intervene. Billy saw him approach, his stride confident and his expression flirtatious. "Well, well, what do we have here?" Pierce purred, placing a possessive hand on Thad's shoulder.

Thad turned to Pierce, a friendly smile still on his face. "Oh, Pierce, did you know Billy was so talented?"

Billy's eyes flickered with annoyance as he glanced at Pierce. "We were in the middle of a conversation, Pierce."

Ignoring Billy, Pierce laid on the charm thickly, determined to shift Thad's attention back to himself. He complimented Thad's attire, his smile dazzling. But when Thad's gaze drifted back to Billy, Pierce's sneer couldn't be concealed.

Chapter 10

It was a Tuesday night nearly a week and a half since Billy and Thad's encounter in the faded grandeur of the Sea Spray Inn lounge, and the days had drifted by like summer itself, filled with the rhythms of life in the coastal town. Despite the passage of time, Pierce couldn't shake the memory of that afternoon, the way Billy and Thad had connected, replaying like a discordant note in his mind.

During this time, Pierce watched Billy find solace in his music, often returning to the grand piano to refine his composition with Thad. Thad's presence had become a source of inspiration for Billy, and Pierce couldn't help but notice how Billy looked forward to their brief interactions.

Yet, the peace in Billy's world was a facade. Pierce's jealousy simmered beneath the surface, threatening to overshadow the growing connection between Billy and Thad. His possessiveness was a constant reminder of the complexities in their intertwined lives.

Pierce's interference became more pronounced each day. He appeared at the most inopportune moments, driven by an underlying desire to keep Billy within his grasp. The atmosphere at the Sea Spray Inn grew tense, with Pierce perceiving an unspoken rivalry between himself and Thad, even though Thad remained blissfully unaware of Pierce's manipulations.

Pierce watched as Billy tried to navigate this delicate situation, balancing his blossoming feelings for Thad with the need to manage Pierce's unpredictable behavior. It was a tightrope walk, fraught with potential misunderstandings and conflicts.

And so, almost two weeks after that afternoon at the piano, the kitchen lay in eerie silence as the moon reflected its paling light over the inn, and Pierce anticipated the next act in his unfolding drama.

The kitchen was dark, save for random strokes of moonlight projecting a film noir eeriness across the floor and against cupboards and hanging pots. The soft glow from a distant streetlamp flickered through the window, casting long, spidery shadows that danced on the walls. A single, cynical, surveilling eye scanned the room through the backdoor window. No one was around; the guests all slept in their rooms, comforted by the cool ocean air and a lullaby of gentle waves on a calm sea.

The door creaked softly as Pierce slipped into the dimly lit kitchen. He moved with the quiet grace of a predator stalking its prey, his jealousy lurking just below the surface. The kitchen, usually bustling with life and noise during the day, now lay silent and still, like a giant beast at rest.

The air was thick with the faint scent of cleaning supplies mingled with the lingering aroma of the day's culinary creations. Stainless steel counters gleamed under the moonlight, reflecting ghostly images of kitchen utensils hanging from hooks above the polished surfaces, creating a surreal scene.

Pierce's narrowed eyes focused on the source of his envy: Billy Pine, his one-time high school classmate and now a line cook, even though Billy was nowhere to be seen. Billy had been fascinated with Thad Lambert, the charming hotel guest who had become a regular at the restaurant. Pierce couldn't bear the thought of Billy's attention being divided between himself and Thad.

As he approached the wooden shelf directly over the range—the one Sarah had complained about and that Billy had repaired—Pierce's thoughts drifted to his father. His father's stern voice echoed in his mind, reminding him of the importance of strength and normalcy. Growing up, Pierce's father, a strict Jamaican man with little patience for anything he perceived as weak or abnormal, had drilled into him the need to conform to traditional masculine norms. Any hint of softness or deviation was met with harsh reprimand. Pierce had learned to bury his true feelings deep inside, masking his vulnerabilities with a facade of control and aggression.

Pierce remembered his father's disdain for anything that deviated from his rigid expectations. "Men don't cry, Pierce. Men don't show weakness," his father would say, his voice as unyielding as stone. These words were more than just lessons; they were commands that shaped Pierce's essence. His father had been a towering figure in his life, both physically and emotionally. The man's presence had loomed over every aspect of Pierce's childhood, casting a long, dark shadow that Pierce could never entirely escape. The constant pressure to meet his father's impossible standards instilled a profound inadequacy in Pierce. He grew up believing that he had to suppress his emotions to survive, to be worthy of his father's begrudging approval.

Pierce's few attempts to show vulnerability were met with scorn and anger. When he'd confided in his father about being bullied at school, hoping for comfort, he was met with a harsh lesson in "manliness." "Stand up for yourself, boy. Don't be weak. Weakness is for the faint-hearted," his father had barked. Pierce learned to mask his pain with bravado, his emotions becoming a tightly coiled spring ready to snap. This suppression led to a need to control his surroundings, a desperate attempt to prove his strength and mask his insecurity.

Pierce had become adept at hiding his emotions, projecting confidence and decisiveness in the kitchen, even as he wrestled with inner turmoil. His father's disapproving voice haunted him, pushing him to assert his authority in any way possible.

The kitchen had become his stage, where he could command respect and admiration. Here, he could bury his insecurities, hiding behind a mask of competence and control. But beneath the surface, the unresolved tensions from his past continued to fester. The sight of Billy and Thad's growing closeness triggered the same feelings of inadequacy and fear of being overshadowed that he had tried so hard to suppress.

Pierce checked the shelf Billy had fixed earlier. It was now firmly in place, the brackets securely fastened with new screws and adhesive. He could see Billy's meticulous work, ensuring the shelf was more stable than ever. Determined to proceed with his plan, Pierce examined the shelf and the brackets more closely, looking for a new way to sabotage it.

Pierce decided to weaken the entire structure. He carefully removed the plates and items from the shelf, setting them aside quietly. He then used a small, flathead screwdriver to loosen the adhesive and pry the brackets slightly away from the wall. Pierce worked methodically, creating just enough instability to make the shelf appear secure but ensuring it would buckle under the weight and jostling of plates during the hectic breakfast service.

As he worked, Pierce couldn't shake the feeling of being watched. He paused and glanced around the darkened kitchen but saw nothing. The sensation of unseen eyes lingered, a prickling at the back of his neck. He brushed it off, attributing it to guilt. But he and guilt were old friends; this feeling was something else, something external, not from within him. He had always felt that his father's disapproving gaze followed him, judging his every move, even in his absence. This pervasive sense of being watched, of never quite measuring up, had become an inescapable part of Pierce's psyche.

Breakfast service was crucial for the hotel's reputation. Pierce knew that if he disrupted it, Billy would be blamed. Then Pierce could sweep in to save the day, win Billy's admiration, and drive Thad away.

As Pierce completed his dark deed, he detected a prick of guilt. This time, he was certain of the feeling. He knew what he was doing was wrong, but his jealousy had consumed him, and he was willing to do anything to reclaim Billy's attention. The conflict between his desire for Billy and the ingrained need to live up to his father's harsh standards created a storm within him.

In moments like these, Pierce could almost hear his father's voice, harsh and unforgiving. "Do what it takes to get ahead, boy. Don't let anyone stand in your way," he would say. But the words that had once driven him now felt like chains, binding him to a life of perpetual conflict and dissatisfaction. Pierce knew that his actions betrayed the person he wanted to be, yet he felt powerless to break free from the cycle of dominance and manipulation his father had instilled in him.

With the trap set, Pierce retreated into the shadows, the

moonlight once again his silent accomplice. The unsettling feeling of being watched remained, but Pierce pushed it aside, too focused on his plan to dwell on it further.

Chapter 11

The Wednesday morning sun bathed the kitchen in a soft, radiant light, casting long shadows across the workspaces as Billy diced shallots on a chopping block. The enticing aroma of bacon crisping in the oven danced with the gentle hiss of water heating up, gradually growing into a soft, continuous hum as it approached a gentle boil, patiently awaiting the moment when eggs would be ordered for poaching. One by one, Sarah, Emily, and Nathan, the wait staff, entered, cheerfully greeting him with a friendly "Good morning!" and "How are you, Billy?" The comforting backdrop of their voices set the stage for a busy day ahead. With a spatula in hand, Billy stood at the ready. When eight o'clock came, everything was in place, and Billy wore a proud smile.

The kitchen was a symphony of sounds and scents. The clatter of utensils and the murmur of early morning chatter created a bustling ambiance, starkly contrasting the serene morning outside. The walls, adorned with pans and shiny utensils, gleamed in the sunlight, reflecting the kitchen's energy and dynamism.

As he settled into his familiar routine, the servers sang out their orders in a chorus that had quickly become second nature. The meal requests were like old habits that clung to the regulars like a comforting security blanket. They'd peruse the menu, ask for suggestions, briefly consider something new, but in the end, they'd always opt for the tried and true. At their age, familiarity was a sanctuary, offering safety and security, something their tired taste buds and delicate stomachs could trust.

However, amidst the usual chorus of "order up," Sarah's unusual order altered the routine.

"Order up, Billy! It's a special request."

"Is it on the menu?'"

"No, but I know you can make it."

Curiosity piqued, Billy inquired, "What is it?"

"It's a green chili omelet, extra spicy."

The request seemed uncharacteristic for the clientele accustomed to milder fare. "Who's it for?" Billy asked as he gathered the ingredients.

"It's for Mr. Lambert. He's so nice, Billy. I told him you'd be happy to make it for him." With a wink, Sarah clipped the order slip to the ticket holder carousel and spun it toward Billy.

Billy had enjoyed interacting with Thad Lambert at the piano the previous night, so he was determined to construct the special omelet. He prepped his ingredients and went to work. In no time at all, he crafted the perfect omelet.

With a plate in one hand and an omelet on the spatula in the other, Billy was ready to slide the concoction onto the plate. Suddenly, a sharp crack broke the rhythmic sounds of the kitchen. The shelf above him—the one he'd repaired on his first day at the hotel—creaked ominously before giving way. The sound of wood splintering and metal clattering filled the air. Plates and bowls crashed onto the grill and burners with a deafening din, shattering into countless fragments. Once a haven of order and routine, the kitchen erupted into chaos like a tornado had swept through, scattering everything in its path.

One large serving platter crashed into the plate Billy was holding, breaking it on contact and scattering its remains around his feet. Porcelain shards, like shrapnel, sprayed in every direction, the sharp pieces reflecting the sunlight in a cruel mimicry of beauty. They penetrated pancakes and eggs; bacon and sausage lay scattered like casualties on a bleak culinary battlefield. The clamor of broken dishes against the tiled floor echoed in the suddenly still kitchen; a cacophony of destruction brought all activity to a standstill.

Gasping for breath but still somehow balancing the unplated omelet on the spatula, Billy scanned the chaos around him, desperately seeking something to mitigate the disaster. His heart pounded in his chest as he looked around at the devastation. The once-orderly kitchen was now a mess of broken dishes and spilled food. Scorched ceramic pieces sliced through the lingering aroma of breakfast, creating a dissonance that spoke of the sudden shift from calm to calamity.

Within moments, all three servers swarmed in, eager to understand what had happened. When Billy turned to address them, the omelet on his spatula slipped and fell to the floor, the final salvo in a short-lived and ill-fated war. Nathan yelled, "Billy, your hand!"

When he looked down, he noticed blood streaked across the front of his chef's jacket, his left hand sliced open across his palm. He dropped the spatula, which joined the aftermath of shattered dishes, creating a red-tinged mosaic of broken fragments. Blood mingled with the shards of porcelain, a stark reminder of the personal toll of the accident. The sight of his blood dripping onto the scattered remains of breakfast was surreal, a moment frozen in time that underscored the sudden and brutal disruption of normalcy. The prospect of serving breakfast to the guests within the hour seemed increasingly doubtful.

As the servers worked to clean up the mess, Emily whispered to Nathan, "Didn't Billy fix that shelf yesterday? Why did it give out so easily?"

Nathan nodded, his eyes wide with confusion. "Yeah, he did. It looked pretty solid to me. I don't get it."

Amidst the chaos, laughter erupted from the other side of the kitchen. Billy turned to see Pierce snickering through a dish towel he'd shoved into his mouth to stifle his laughter. The prankster stood in his usual spot, offering neither assistance nor sympathy.

Billy's mind roiled` in a cauldron of hot and fierce anger. He'd been betrayed. How could Pierce find amusement in this disaster? The thought of how much care he had put into Thad's omelet made his stomach churn. Billy had always strived to maintain a professional demeanor, but Pierce's constant undermining had finally worn him down. This wasn't just a mistake but a calculated move to humiliate him and derail his hard work.

Billy stood frozen, his face a mask of shock and disbelief. He grabbed a clean dish towel and haphazardly wrapped it around his wounded hand. Pierce remained a silent spectator, offering no help as Sarah and Emily scrambled to clean up the mess while Nathan ran for the first aid kit. A thousand thoughts raced through Billy's mind: his pride in his work, the respect he had earned from his colleagues, and the growing admiration he felt for Thad all unraveled before his eyes, undone by a single act of spite.

Billy's heart pounded in his chest as he glanced at Pierce.

His anger coiled tighter and tighter within him, like a spring wound to its limit. Memories of all the subtle jabs, condescending remarks, and deliberate sabotage flooded back, each a fresh wound like the cut on his hand. He had always tried to see the best in people, but Pierce had crossed a line. Like that coiled spring, Billy's resolve could only take so much tension before it snapped, seeking release. He could feel that moment approaching, the breaking point where all the pent-up frustration and hurt would erupt uncontrollably.

Billy's frustration and anger reached a boiling point, and he turned to Pierce with a furious glare.

"You!" Billy shouted, his voice filled with rage. "This is your fault, Pierce! You stood there and did nothing!"

Pierce's lips curled into a sly smile. Was he relishing the moment? "Oh, Billy, don't be so quick to blame me. Accidents happen, you know." He then noticed the towel covering Billy's hand as it continued to absorb the blood from the wound.

"Billy, I'm so…"

But Billy was not in the mood for excuses. His face flushed with anger, and he pointed a trembling finger at Pierce before he could complete his apology. As Billy looked at Pierce, he saw not just a coworker and former classmate but a symbol of every obstacle and challenge he had faced. The years of trying to prove himself and the relentless effort to rise above culminated in this moment.

The realization hit him like a wave: staying in this toxic environment was a losing battle. No amount of hard work or dedication could overcome the malice and jealousy plaguing this place. He thought of his dreams, his aspirations for his future, and how the constant undermining stifled them. Quitting wasn't just an escape; it was a declaration of his worth and a refusal to be dragged down further.

"You said you'd have my back if something went wrong. I've had enough of your games and your attitude, Pierce. I quit!"

The words hung in the air, leaving the kitchen staff stunned as Billy stormed out. As he walked away, he felt liberated. The decision to quit was not just an impulsive reaction to Pierce's sabotage but a step toward reclaiming his self-respect and integrity. Billy knew that by leaving, he was opening the door to new possibilities, ones where he could find the respect and appreciation he deserved.

Chapter 12

Standing alone in the shadow of the kitchen's back door as Sarah, Nathan, and Emily continued cleaning up the mess, his regret was tangible, burdening him as it had on that winter morning many years ago. Pierce savored a twisted satisfaction as the kitchen's chaos subsided. His plan to get back at Billy for stealing Thad's attention when Billy's focus should be solely on him was well underway, and he was resolved to see it through to completion. However, Billy cutting his hand wasn't part of the equation.

And then the look on Billy's face. Shock, anger, and finally disappointment. That hurt. He remembered the first time he'd seen it on Billy years ago in high school, standing at the river's edge, the frigid air biting his cheeks. Now, the scene returned as if watching a severe close-up of Billy's distraught face, playing over and over, a relentless loop that tightened around his chest with each iteration. He hadn't been able to shake off the image of Billy's desperate eyes, the panic in his voice as he called out for Finn, his dog, slipping away beneath the ice.

The memory of that day stung like a thorn permanently lodged in Pierce's mind, an ever-present reminder of his failures. Billy's eyes, wide with fear, had looked straight into his own, pleading for help. Pierce had felt a surge of panic and guilt, a rare flicker of empathy that clashed with the mocking laughter of his friends Karl and Jake. They were The Posse, a group bound by an unspoken code of dominance and ridicule, a brotherhood where any sign of weakness was ruthlessly exploited. Pierce felt pressured to conform and maintain his standing within the group, even if it meant disregarding Billy's suffering.

The laughter and camaraderie of his friends felt hollow now, their verbal jabs and taunts a distant echo that he wished he could silence. Pierce had always been a part of The Posse, never questioning, always following, but the incident with Billy and Finn had fractured something within him.

He had looked to his friends, hoping they'd understand and join him in helping. But they hadn't. They'd laughed it off, dragging him away from the one moment he might have made a difference. That day, Pierce had realized his friends' shallow cruelty, but he lacked the courage to stand against them. The laughter that had once bonded them now felt like chains, binding him to a past he was ashamed of.

Pierce wished he could go back, wished he had acted differently. He could have broken ranks with Karl and Jake, offered a hand to Billy, and maybe even saved Finn. But he hadn't. He'd chosen silence, chosen loyalty to friends who, at that moment, had shown they were not worthy of it.

The image of Billy's disappointment from that day lingered in his mind. The guilt gnawed at him, a constant, unyielding companion. The thought that he had again caused Billy harm, even unintentionally, made his chest ache with a familiar, bitter regret.

If Pierce noticed Sarah's eyes darting towards him every few seconds, he didn't let on. He tried to appear oblivious to her and the other servers' presence, focusing instead on kicking at the door jamb—a futile attempt to alleviate the remorse weighing heavily on him. Inevitably, he stubbed his toe. The sharp pain was a welcome distraction from the dull ache of guilt, a small penance for the enormous wrongs he felt unable to rectify. He couldn't stop wondering if Billy would ever forgive him or if he could ever forgive himself. Why hadn't he rushed in to save the day as he had planned when he first conceived of loosening the shelf bracket?

"Hey, chef?" Sarah approached Pierce, her tone firm but understanding. "We've got to salvage the breakfast service somehow. You'll have to cook if Billy's not coming back. Hungry guests are waiting."

Pierce reluctantly joined the effort but was mired in the realization that every time he had stood by, laughed along, or looked the other way, he could've done something to help. The loss of Billy's dog had become a symbol of all the moments Pierce had let pass by, moments when he could have been kinder, braver, and better.

Pierce's thoughts turned to Billy, who had always been the bright, kind-hearted boy, the one who never seemed to let life's hardships dim his spirit. Billy's resilience had been both a source of fascination and irritation for Pierce. Deep down, he admired Billy's strength and how he kept going despite the odds, but he had never known how to express that admiration without feeling vulnerable. His upbringing taught him to mask any sign of weakness and hide behind a facade of control and indifference.

Pierce made a decision. He couldn't undo the past, but he could shape his future. He would start by apologizing to Billy, even if it meant that facing his shame would lead to the possibility of rejection. It wouldn't bring Finn back or undo the cut on Billy's hand, but it could be a step toward mending the rift his actions had caused. He'd find Billy and confess. The stakes were high; this wasn't just about an apology. It was about proving to himself that he could be better, that he could step out from the shadows of his past and take responsibility for his actions. But first, he needed to cook breakfast for guests who hadn't fled the dining room. He felt lighter as he walked back into the kitchen despite the limp from stubbing his toe. This decision to face his guilt and seek forgiveness was a new kind of courage for him, a step toward breaking free from the cycle of shame and regret that had defined his life. It was a small comfort, but was it enough to set things straight with Billy? If he could deliver his apology properly, maybe he'd even get Billy to return to work. He needed him.

Chapter 13

Billy descended the warped back steps and crossed the crushed shell driveway to the bunkhouse, the dorm-like wooden structure behind the hotel that housed staff. He had a cot there, though he rarely slept in it since his home was a leisurely bike ride away. Instead, when on duty, he used the room to store his backpack and a few personal items, like a change of clothes and a bathing suit. Sarah rushed after him, drying her hands on a dishtowel.

"Billy, can I talk to you for a second?" she asked, her voice low and urgent.

"Sure, Sarah. What's up?" Billy replied, still feeling the sting of the morning's events and cradling his hand.

"I need to tell you something about what happened last night. I saw Pierce in the kitchen. At first, I thought he was admiring the work you had done on that shelf we've all complained about, but now I realize he was tampering with it. He rigged it to fall during breakfast."

Billy stared at her, processing the revelation. "You saw him do it?"

Sarah nodded, her expression serious. "I didn't understand what he was doing at the time. But after what happened this morning, there's no denying it."

A surge of anger washed over him. He had always tried to

see the best in people, to give them the benefit of the doubt, but this? This was a calculated act of sabotage. He had trusted Pierce, hoping their shared past might mend old wounds. Now, those hopes seemed foolishly misplaced.

"Does he know you saw him?" Billy's voice was tight, barely concealing his anger.

"He didn't know I was there. It was late, and I couldn't sleep, so I began folding napkins for this morning's service. I was sitting in the dark by the pantry. I didn't say anything because I didn't want him asking why I was there or giving me extra chores. Pierce can come up with tasks when you least expect it."

"Why didn't you tell me sooner?"

"I didn't put it together until now," Sarah explained. "I thought he was helping, not sabotaging. I'm so sorry, Billy."

Billy took a deep breath, trying to calm the storm of emotions inside him. He was angry at Pierce for his deceit and frustrated with himself for not seeing through Pierce's facade sooner.

"Thank you for telling me, Sarah. It means a lot. I'll handle this."

"You're not quitting, Billy, are you? We need you here; you make things so much better."

Billy's heart ached at the sincerity in Sarah's voice. He loved the camaraderie of the kitchen and knew he had a purpose in cooking for the guests. Yet, the thought of continuing to work alongside Pierce, knowing what he had done, filled him with dread. He weighed the decision in his mind, the pros and cons swirling together in a chaotic dance.

"Sorry, Sarah, but he's too much for me. We have a history together that's less than positive. I could use the money, but I also thought it would improve things between Pierce and me. I was wrong."

"Okay, Billy, I get it. We'll miss you. We'll come to La Péniche some night to hear you play."

Billy forced a smile, but inside, his heart was heavy. Leaving the hotel felt like admitting defeat, but he knew it was the right choice. He needed to protect his peace of mind and his integrity. The prospect of seeing his friends outside of work, away from Pierce's toxic influence, offered a small measure of comfort.

"All right, Sarah. See you around, and thanks for all your help getting me up to speed in the kitchen when I started."

With newfound determination, Billy realized he had to confront Pierce again, but this time with the truth. He couldn't let Pierce's actions go unchallenged. He had to stand up for himself and ensure that justice was served.

Billy walked into the bunkhouse, feeling both resignation and resolve. Leaving the hotel meant giving up a steady income and a chance to be closer to Thad, but staying would mean sacrificing his self-respect. He replayed the morning's events in his mind—the sound of the shelf crashing down, the sight of his blood mixing with the shattered porcelain, and Pierce's cruel laughter echoing in the background. Each recollection solidified his decision to leave.

He grabbed his belongings from his room and headed to the communal bathroom. He discarded the thoroughly stained and soggy towel, tossing it into the trash bin along with his chef's jacket. His hand throbbed, and he closed his eyes, not wanting to deal with the injury until he had washed off some of the blood. Taking a deep breath, he opened his eyes, expecting to see the end of his piano playing. To his surprise, the cut, running diagonally from just below his index finger to near his wrist, was clean and skin-deep—a perfect slice with no jagged edges or porcelain fragments, no tendons damaged. He wiggled his fingers to confirm it. He'd be fine, although he'd need to dress the wound properly once he got home. Grabbing a few paper towels, he jury-rigged a temporary bandage. He pulled the stretchy hair tie from his short ponytail, secured it around the paper towels to keep them in place, and left.

Chapter 14

Billy dressed his wound, then dressed himself. With one hand out of commission, he struggled to change into his bathing trunks, the snug, navy fabric hugging his thighs as he coaxed them into place. The suit clung to his athletic frame, accentuating the contours of his tan skin. He ran a hand through his shaggy blond hair, the contrast against his deep navy suit adding to the casual yet striking look. Fetching a fresh white T-shirt from his backpack, he slipped into it with a slight shiver, then pinned the beach badge to the waistband of his suit. As he adjusted it, the stretchy waistband snapped back against his skin with a taut, almost electric sensation, hugging low on his hips, its elastic edge teasingly tracing a line around his midsection.

He packed the rest of his belongings. He dragged his baseball cap across his scalp and left the barracks. Feeling caged after the incident, craving fresh air and space, he needed to clear his head before returning home. With every step he took, the betrayal from Pierce gnawed at him, tightening around his heart, making each breath a heavy chore. He kept asking himself why Pierce hadn't come over to help him when the shelf gave way and massacred the breakfast of innocent hotel guests. Didn't he care about the guests waiting for their meals that would never arrive at their tables? It was his kitchen, after all. Did he not care?

The questions swirled in his mind like a relentless Nor'easter. Why had Pierce chosen to sabotage him? Was it simple jealousy, or was there something more profound? Billy's thoughts drifted to their shared past, the moments of camaraderie and competition, the unspoken tension that had always simmered between them. The realization that envy and resentment had driven Pierce's actions cut deeper than the wound on his hand.

Outside, he unlocked his bicycle, jumped on, and pedaled across the street to the beach. Here, he intended to spend the rest of the day finding solace in the sun's soothing warmth and the hypnotic rhythm of the waves. He dropped his bike, pulled out the beach towel in his backpack, and spread it over the sand. He squirmed out of his T-shirt and stretched out on his back, carefully keeping his injured hand out of the sand. The sun's rays instantly released the tension in his body. He closed his eyes.

The beach was a sanctuary, a place where he could escape the chaos of the kitchen and the turmoil of his thoughts. The rhythmic sound of the waves crashing against the shore provided a soothing backdrop, a reminder that the world continued to turn, even as his life unraveled. He focused on the benefits of his decision—escaping the toxic environment of the kitchen would bring tranquility into his life and provide more time to dedicate to his music.

A lifeguard, returning from his break, passed Billy sunbathing and noticed his hand wrapped in paper towels; thin streaks of blood covered the quilted paper. The guard knelt beside Billy and gently tapped on his shoulder.

"Excuse me, what's up with your hand? Looks like it's

bleeding. What kind of bandage is that?"

Billy opened one eye. A shirtless man in red square-cut swim briefs came into focus. Billy's other eye shot open. Not a dream, but dreamlike.

"Hi! Um…yeah, I cut myself this morning. Broken plate. It doesn't look too bad, and I'll do a proper bandage when I get home later."

"You know what? Let me fix that up for you. Come over to my post. I've got a first aid kit. I'll clean it up for you and put on a real bandage."

Billy followed him back to his elevated lifeguard chair, enjoying the unobstructed view of the well-built man as he barefooted through the sand in his skintight trunks. GUARD was emblazoned across the back, accentuating his well-muscled butt and giving Billy a sudden rush.

Billy felt a slight relief as they walked. The lifeguard's casual kindness contrasted starkly with the destructive drama he had left behind at the hotel. It was a reminder that there were still good people in the world, people who cared without expecting anything in return. This simple act of assistance felt like a balm for his weary soul.

The guard cleaned Billy's wound, applied antibiotic cream, and wrapped his hand in a waterproof, stretchy gauze adhesive bandage. Billy thanked him and returned to his towel to relax some more.

As Billy settled back onto his towel, the lifeguard's gesture of kindness and the sun's steady presence lifted some of the weight from his shoulders. He realized that while he couldn't change the past or Pierce's actions, he could control how he responded to them. He decided to take this time to focus on himself, to find peace and clarity in the rhythmic crashing of the waves and the way the sand cushioned his body.

Billy decided not to return the beach badge when he'd eventually go see Ron Service to collect his back pay. The tag would become his symbolic severance, a token of his escape from the culinary chaos and Pierce. He resolved to make the most of the summer, embracing the freedom ahead. He'd survive this. He was thankful he had enough savings to make it through the next few weeks, though barely. He had his gig at La Péniche, at least through Labor Day when the upstairs lounge closed for the season. But most of all, his dignity was intact. His only regret was not being able to see Thad, but he'd get over that. Thad would eventually return to his life in New York, and Billy would be back in the classroom soon enough. If there was a glimmer of romance between them hidden under their mutual love of music, it didn't matter, he figured, especially with Pierce seemingly blocking every move they made to spend time together. If Billy was only interested in finding someone to love, plenty of other fish were in the sea at the Jersey Shore.

Billy's thoughts drifted to Thad and the brief moments they had shared. He felt sad about what could have been but also relieved. The drama with Pierce had shown him that he needed to focus on his well-being first to build a life free from manipulation and deceit. He'd put his romantic notions with Thad on hold until he could unmuddle his brain from his current situation and find clarity within himself.

The sun and sand did their magic, and Billy drifted off. He stirred slightly when a coolness washed over him. He imagined a cloud drifting across the sky, temporarily blocking the sun. Or did his hero lifeguard come back for his phone number? He opened his eyes to check, and through his squint, he discerned the outline of a man standing over him.

Billy blinked against the bright light, lifting a hand to shade his face. His eyebrows furrowed as he tried to make out the figure.

Pierce crouched next to Billy, still in his kitchen whites, blending in with the day's brilliance. Billy adjusted the baseball cap to better shield his eyes from the sharpness of the noonday sun. He propped himself up on his elbows and glared at Pierce.

Pierce whimpered, his eyes darted nervously, and his fingers fidgeting with the hem of his jacket. He glanced down, avoiding Billy's intense gaze.

"I'm so sorry, Billy. I should have stepped in to help, but that shelf falling like that, especially after the repair job you did on it, took me by surprise. I should have done something. How's your hand?"

Billy sat up fully, wincing slightly as he shifted his weight. He flexed his hand, showing the bandage.

"You're sorry? You're something else, Pierce. You know that? I know what you did, tampering with that old shelf above the cooktop—the one you had me repair on the first day I came to work in the kitchen. I know, Pierce, and I'm so disappointed in you."

Billy's lips curled into a sneer, his nostrils flaring. Pierce's shoulders slumped, his face paling.

Billy was angry. He had come to the beach to escape, to find some peace, and now Pierce was here, dredging up all the bitterness he had tried to leave behind.

Billy clenched his fists, the tendons in his neck standing out as he tried to control his breathing. Pierce shifted uncomfortably, his eyes darting to the side.

"As for my hand, it'll be fine; nothing for you to worry about. And Pierce, you could've done something. You said you had my back. And what's worse, you just stood there and laughed like it was some weird punchline to a poorly timed prank."

Billy's voice cracked slightly with the intensity of his emotions. Pierce flinched at the accusation, his mouth opening and closing as if searching for words.

"I just told you I'm sorry. Come back to the kitchen with me, and we can discuss it. You're doing a great job, so I'm not looking for someone else. Come on, Billy, we're friends."

Pierce extended a hand tentatively, his eyes pleading. Billy shook his head, eyes narrowing further.

Billy's frustration boiled over. Pierce wouldn't even admit to his act of sabotage. The casual way Pierce talked about their friendship, as if the morning's events hadn't happened, felt like a slap in the face.

Billy's jaw tightened, a muscle twitching in his cheek. He crossed his arms over his chest, shifting slightly to sit up straighter.

"You annoy the hell out of me. Like whenever I have a moment's rest or attempt to play the hotel's piano, which, you remember, you offered me as a perk when I'm not working in the kitchen, you invent some excuse to keep me near you. And what's with you always showing up anytime I talk with someone other than the servers and staff?"

Pierce's eyes widened, and he recoiled slightly, his hand dropping. "You mean Thad?" His voice was a whisper, and his eyes widened with fear.

"Yes, I mean Thad! What is it with you?" Billy's voice rose, and he jabbed a finger in Pierce's direction, his face flushed with anger.

"I don't want you talking with the guests." Pierce's face hardened, his posture stiffening defensively.

Billy leaned forward, eyes boring into Pierce's, daring him to lie. "Do you mean the guests or just Thad?"

"I like you, Billy." Pierce's voice broke, and he bit his lip, his eyes glistening. "I have since high school."

"You have a strange way of showing me." Billy's eyebrows shot up, and he shook his head incredulously.

"Yeah, I've been a shit at times, not just to you. But I'm trying here. I like you; we're good together." Pierce's voice was earnest, his eyes locking onto Billy's with a desperate intensity.

"Wait a minute... are you talking about in the kitchen or something more?" Billy's eyes widened, and he stared at Pierce in disbelief. "Are you telling me you like me, like me? I thought you were just a chronic flirt. Men or women, it doesn't seem to matter to you. Is your ego that hungry for attention, or are you just trying to manipulate me, or is this some weird game all just for fun?"

Pierce's face flushed, and he looked away, his shoulders sagging. "Billy..." Pierce's voice wavered, and his gaze was heavy and wet.

Pierce's sudden confession left Billy reeling. The revelation of affection cloaked in jealousy sent a dizzying shock through him. He combed his fingers through his hair, his gaze fixed unwaveringly on Pierce. "You know what, Pierce? I don't have time for this. I'm not going back with you. If I want to cook, I'll cook for my friends. I don't need this. I thought I was doing a good deed for you, but now I see I was wrong. Tell Ron I'll be around tomorrow to pick up my pay."

Billy's voice was firm. He stood up, brushing sand off

himself. Pierce's hand reached out as if to stop him but fell back limply.

Before Pierce could respond, Billy headed for the ocean. He waded in a bit, and on the first breaking wave, he dove in and began swimming, hoping the bandage would live up to its waterproof guarantee. Billy's strokes were powerful and steady, each one propelling him further from the shore and the turmoil of his emotions. As he cut through the water, the cool embrace of the ocean began to wash away the heat of his anger, leaving clarity in its wake. He realized he had made the right decision to leave, to forge his path free from Pierce's toxic influence.

When he finally released the last trace of his anger, he swam back toward the shore and noticed Pierce was still watching him. Billy emerged from the ocean, his silhouette in stark contrast against the breaking blue-green waves behind him. Water droplets cascaded down his toned physique as he strode purposefully back to his spot on the sand. As he got closer, Pierce turned away and retreated off the beach. Billy watched him cross the highway to the hotel.

Billy felt a bittersweet closure as he watched Pierce disappear. He had confronted his past, faced the demons that had haunted him, and come out the other side stronger and more resilient. The path ahead was uncertain, but he felt hopeful for the first time in a long while. With its vast expanse of sand and sea, the beach stretched before him, a blank canvas waiting to be filled with the colors of his new freedom.

He lay back down on his towel and closed his eyes again. The rhythmic sound of the waves crashing onto the shore became a soothing lullaby, easing the tension from his body and mind. The thought of returning to La Péniche, focusing on his music, and leaving behind the soiled atmosphere of the hotel filled him with a renewed purpose.

Billy's mind wandered to the future, envisioning the possibilities ahead. He thought about the gigs at La Péniche, the familiar comfort of the piano keys under his fingers, and the joy of creating music that touched people's lives. He imagined reconnecting with friends, finding new opportunities, and perhaps discovering love in a more supportive and nurturing environment.

A soft voice interrupted his thoughts. "Hey, you all right?"

Billy opened his eyes to see the lifeguard standing over him again, concern etched on his face. "Yeah, I'm okay. Just needed a moment to clear my head."

The lifeguard knelt beside him, eyes scanning Billy's face with genuine concern. "You seemed a bit out of it earlier. If you need anything, let me know. I'm here to help."

The lifeguard's sincerity touched Billy. In a world where he often felt alone, it was reassuring to know there were still people who cared.

"Thanks. I really appreciate it. It was a rough morning."

"Sounds like you had quite a day. If you ever want to talk, I'm here. By the way, I'm Noah."

"Billy. Nice to meet you, Noah. Thanks for helping with my hand earlier."

"Anytime, Billy. Take care of yourself."

Noah jogged back to his post, leaving Billy feeling hopeful.

Billy shook the sand out of his towel, gathered the rest of his belongings, and returned to his bike. He rode home with the sea breeze pushing against his back, feeling lighter than he had in a long time. The day's events had been a turning point, a moment of clarity that had given him strength.

At home, he put away his bike and tended to his hand, cleaning the wound and applied a fresh bandage.

Curious about how his injured hand would fare on the piano, he lightly touched the keys. He played a few notes, letting the music flow through him, a cathartic release of the day's emotions. He discovered he could play with minimal discomfort, his dexterity intact. Closing the piano lid, a small smile appeared on his lips.

Chapter 15

Billy's decision to quit his job at the Sea Spray Inn had been bold but ultimately a good one. Who needed that kind of drama? With La Péniche as his only source of income for the remainder of the summer and his hand making good progress—despite the occasional itch reminding him of the cut and the treachery behind it—he knew he had to put in extra effort to make ends meet. The cozy little bar was packed almost every night. The audience couldn't get enough of Billy's music, and the sound of their applause, mingling with the virtuosity of his piano playing, filled his heart with a joy that made all his worries disappear. He poured his soul into every note, the music carrying the weight of his dreams and loss. Since teaming up with Viktoria, he saw an almost daily increase in the tip jar; sometimes they emptied its contents a few times a night to make room for more. This ensured he could continue pursuing his passion through the summer. He soon realized he wouldn't miss the extra income from his short stint as a cook.

And now Billy had time to complete the composition he'd been working on. He'd learned to be patient, sometimes for hours, trusting his muse to ignite a memory, a feeling he could capture as he turned sound into visual art. For him, sounds attached themselves to each of his memories on vibrating golden threads. It was akin to synesthesia, how some musicians see colors when they hear sounds. For Billy, all the music already existed in his head. All he had to do was identify the corresponding golden thread and capture it in pen and ink. He took pride in the precision of each stroke, with each note flowing seamlessly to the next—each crucial to the beauty and clarity of the manuscript. Who knew who might someday stumble across one of his compositions? He wanted them to look as good as they sounded.

Billy committed to returning daily to the unfinished piece he had played for Thad at the Sea Spray Inn. He was on the brink of completion, but the thread of the ever-ethereal coda seemed to vanish like mist, slipping through his fingers each time he attempted to capture it in the final section. It was as though the thread leading to the coda was always out of reach, reluctant to leave its safe place, fearing it would be forgotten forever once woven into the music and brought out into the open. It felt like completing the composition would replace the memory, which in turn had replaced the life that was taken, escaping through a crack in the window like a departing soul at the moment of death.

Billy had even considered asking Thad for help. Thad could offer a suggestion or insight on concluding the piece. But after what had happened yesterday in the kitchen, that was out of the question. Billy's hand throbbed at the mere thought of it.

Billy rarely spoke about the memory he was trying to mine, a buried ore that, once refined, would reveal the elusive coda. Despite his father spending thousands on therapy following the incident with Finn, the memory remained tightly bundled in his mind, leaving him to struggle in silence. The therapist had encouraged Billy to use his creativity as a way to process his grief. The strategy sometimes proved successful, but now he felt stuck. He wanted to force the golden thread free and yank it into the open, but he also didn't want to damage it by pulling it out before it was ready.

Billy opened a living room window for fresh air. Even this far from the beach, an ocean breeze entered the apartment. He sat back down at the piano.

Billy played the piece from the beginning, hoping that by the time he reached the place where the coda should begin, he'd be inspired—or rather, his muse would coax out the ending just waiting to emerge from Billy's memory.

He began to play. The opening section bounced with athletic agility—playful and carefree, slightly disarming as it lulled you into a pleasant reverie of childhood games and spontaneity. The shift came unexpectedly; atonal madness stretched over the piano keys, almost as if Billy used his elbows, forearms, and fists to make his point. His left hand throbbed as the segue took hold. A fermataed silence, intentionally prolonged until a listener became uncomfortable and questioned whether the piece had ended or the pianist had quit midway through, served as the staging area to launch a poignant melody, filling the space with ghostly tonal apparitions. Notes rose and fell in a gentle cadence, painting a soundscape of both sorrow and transcendence—a wistful grace.

The composition unfolded like a spectral ballet, its rhythmic qualities pushing and pulling against each other with the rubato of ebbing and flowing tides. Carefully placed diminuendos and crescendos contrasted masterfully between quiet passages and forceful swells of sound, creating spaces for reflection and introspection, like the difference between flat and rough seas.

And then nothing. Here was where the coda began, but Billy had nothing. His muse shrugged, and the memory stilled. Maybe next time.

Chapter 16

Thad couldn't shake the memory of his encounters with Billy at the Sea Spray Inn. He was drawn to the talented pianist who seemed to understand music in a way that resonated with his soul. It was Friday morning, and he wondered why Billy hadn't been at the hotel for two days. Thad wanted to continue their conversation, learn more about Billy and his music, and, most importantly, discover his whereabouts.

Thad entered the hotel's dining room, ordered the chef's special: seared scallops on perfectly made risotto, and dug in. As Pierce made his rounds to each table, talking to the guests as chefs sometimes do, Thad couldn't contain his curiosity. When the chef reached his table, Thad asked, "Excuse me, Pierce, do you know what happened to Billy? I haven't seen him in two days."

Pierce knelt next to Thad, who had his reasons for keeping Billy's departure a secret, and decided to tread lightly. "Oh, Billy," he said with a hint of sadness. "Well, you see, he had some personal matters to attend to and had to leave the hotel. It was quite sudden."

"Is he coming back?"

"I don't think so."

Thad frowned, disappointment etched on his face. "That's a shame," he murmured. "He made a great breakfast." Except for a few days ago, when his breakfast took forever and wasn't what he ordered. A server had apologized, mentioning trouble in the kitchen. Now that he thought about it, Thad hadn't seen Billy at all during or after that meal.

"Yes, that boy could cook," Pierce confirmed.

"But I hoped to get to know him better. I'm heading back to the city tomorrow, and I have a planning meeting with the dance company next week, so I guess that won't happen."

Pierce nodded sympathetically, and Thad sensed he was hearing half-truths from the chef as if he was keeping Billy's departure a secret. He sensed something was off; Pierce was holding back, and he'd probably learn nothing more about Billy's sudden disappearance.

After dinner, Thad approached Ron Service, the hotel manager. He'd heard a few hotel guests mention a nearby bar that had live music. He thought going out for the evening would be good and queried Ron.

"Ron, I've heard about this local piano bar. Do you know where it is?"

Ron smiled knowingly. "La Péniche is just a short walk from here in Beachside. It's above The Barge. You can't miss it."

Thad thanked Ron, stepped onto the veranda, and began walking toward the bar. He knew The Barge and had eaten there numerous times but had no idea there was a piano bar on the second floor. He also had no idea what he'd soon discover once he crossed La Péniche's threshold.

Chapter 17

Pierce lingered in the shadows of the dining room, his heart pounding as he strained to hear the conversation between Thad and Ron. He listened more intently when Ron told Thad about La Péniche. While Pierce had promised himself to control his emotions regarding Billy, he was concerned about what would happen when Thad discovered Billy playing piano at the nearby bar. He feared that a bond was forming between the two musicians, and he couldn't stand by and watch them grow closer, not if he ever wanted to reconcile with Billy after what he'd done.

Pierce yearned for Billy, but the idea of seeing Thad and Billy together was unbearable. If Pierce couldn't have Billy, then neither could Thad.

He watched as Thad crossed the verandah and walked along Ocean Boulevard headed for La Péniche, and a surge of determination swept over him. He knew exactly what his next move had to be to keep the distance between the two musicians intact. He would need to play a dangerous game requiring cunning and subtlety. He couldn't afford another overt failure like the kitchen incident.

As he turned back toward the kitchen, Pierce recalled the night he first ran into Billy at La Péniche. Despite his foul mood that night after his line cook quit, the intimate setting, filled with the soft murmur of patrons and the gentle clinking of glasses, had made him feel hopeful. Seeing Billy at the piano, pouring his heart into the music, had rekindled the feelings Pierce had buried since high school. Back then, he had admired Billy from afar, never daring to voice his feelings due to the fear instilled by his father's harsh expectations and the judgment of his friends, especially Jake and Karl.

Approaching Billy that night had been a leap of faith. Pierce had hoped to reconnect, to perhaps find a way into Billy's life. But his jealousy and insecurities had driven him to actions that now seemed foolish. His scheme to sabotage the breakfast service was meant to draw Billy closer, to make him rely on Pierce. Instead, it had pushed Billy away.

Pierce clenched his fists, his resolve hardening. He would have to be more strategic. His goal was to create friction between Thad and Billy, to make Thad seem unreliable or insincere in Billy's eyes. He couldn't afford another confrontation; he needed to be subtle, planting seeds of doubt and mistrust.

He knew enough about Thad's life in the city: his work with a major dance company and being surrounded by dancers, some of whom, he imagined, were hot and interested in Thad. He and Thad got along well during his stay at the hotel. He'd use that friendliness tonight and make a concerted effort to befriend Thad. He'd approached him several times in the common room when Thad was at the piano, complimenting his playing and showing a genuine interest in his work with the dance company. Thad, always gracious, seemed to welcome Pierce's interest, and soon, Pierce had learned enough about Thad's upcoming projects, his struggles with a newly commissioned composition, and his dedication to the dance company. Pierce had listened intently, and he'd use it all in formulating his plan, especially Thad's concern with a male dancer—he thought his name was Liam something or other—and needing that new work for the fall season. Then, Pierce could casually mention to Billy how dedicated Thad was to his work and how he was attracted to the young, hot dancer. He'd paint a picture of Thad as someone whose priorities might not always align with Billy's.

He pictured himself telling Billy, "Thad's a great guy, but you know, his work keeps him in the city unless the company's on tour to who knows where and for how long." Pierce would say, his tone seemingly innocent. "Sounds glamorous. He also told me all about this guy, Liam, and how he needed to get back to the city to be with him. Maybe they're an item." He imagined Billy listening to him, his expression thoughtful until doubt took root, making Billy question Thad's reliability without appearing malicious.

Pierce decided to hold off on finishing the remaining kitchen chores until the morning. He went to the bunkhouse behind the hotel, showered, put on a fresh shirt, tight jeans, and loafers, and headed to La Péniche.

Chapter 18

It was Friday night at La Péniche. Billy was in the middle of his set, filling the room with the enchanting melodies that had made him a local sensation. Viktoria Sinclair, martini in hand, balanced on the barstool next to him. As Billy slid into a Gershwin-esque intro and vamped, Viktoria set her drink on the piano, took the mic from its stand, and waited for the audience to settle before belting out a scathing rendition of "The Man That Got Away." Her powerful voice captivated the audience, and her dramatic performance left everyone in awe.

Amidst the applause and laughter, Thad entered and ordered a drink at the bar, his eyes scanning the room until they settled on an empty stool at the piano's edge. To his surprise, he spotted Billy at the piano, his fingers dancing gracefully across the keys. Billy's left hand tingled, but the sharp pain from the cut had eased. He noticed Thad and smiled, his expression tender and genuine, lighting up the room.

After Viktoria's show-stopping number, Billy took a break from playing and approached Thad, with Viktoria trailing nearby. He was intrigued by Thad's presence. "Hey there," he greeted Thad, his eyes sparkling with interest. "What brings you here tonight?"

Captivated by Billy's charisma and enchanting music, Thad confessed, "I've heard rumors about this fabulous piano player, and I just had to come see for myself."

Viktoria, always the life of the party, chimed in, showering Billy with praise. "Oh, darling, you've stumbled upon a true gem. Billy here is not just incredibly talented; he's also one of the sweetest people you'll ever meet."

The three of them continued to talk through Billy's break, sharing stories and laughter as the night unfolded.

As Billy returned to the piano for his next set, the patrons in the bar grew lively. They called out song titles, and someone asked Billy if he knew "I Fall in Love Too Easily," a Jule Styne and Sammy Cahn song from *Anchors Aweigh*. The woman who requested it joined Billy at the piano as she grabbed the mic to sing. Viktoria leaned over to Billy and whispered, "She's singing your song, Billy."

Billy side-eyed her and then grinned. When the woman finished, Billy turned toward Thad and asked, "Would you like to play a tune?"

Thad accepted the invitation and sat on the piano bench as Billy moved aside. With a puckish glint, Billy grabbed the microphone to address the audience, "Ladies and gentlemen, we have a guest performer joining us tonight. Please welcome all the way from Manhattan, the talented Thad Lambert."

Applause followed as Thad began to play a hyper-stylized rendition of Fats Waller's "Ain't Misbehavin." The audience grew silent, drawn in by the guest at the piano. The moment was disrupted when the door of La Péniche opened, and Pierce walked in.

Pierce bought a drink and sauntered over to Billy's seat. He leaned in close, whispering, "Even though you're no longer working for me, Billy Boy, I wanted to stop by and see how you were making out."

"Go away, Pierce; I don't have time for this tonight."

"Okay, Billy. I only wanted to say hi and give you a heads-up about your crush, Thad."

Billy straightened up, every muscle tensed. "Go away, I said. I'm not interested in anything you have to say."

Pierce mentioned something about Thad having a boyfriend in the city, which Billy only partially heard over the music before moving to stand next to Thad at the piano. Thad smiled at Pierce, showing his friendly nature. Pierce then whispered something only Thad could hear, and both men turned their gaze toward Billy, who couldn't hide his displeasure.

Billy couldn't shake the jealousy that washed over him, even though he didn't quite understand its source. Pierce winked at him, flashed a sly smile, and casually placed a possessive hand on Thad's shoulder.

Billy, determined not to let Pierce's presence ruin the night, returned to the piano to finish his set. Thad reclaimed his seat to enjoy the music. But Pierce stayed behind, sitting beside Billy on the piano bench.

Leaning in close, Pierce taunted, "How does that feel, Billy Boy? You don't even realize how much you're into him. But I'm not going to let that happen."

Billy was so furious with Pierce that he tried to shove him off the bench, but with his athletic build and firm grip, he refused to budge, maintaining his predatory position next to Billy.

Viktoria, keenly aware of what Pierce could do to make Billy's life miserable, observed the situation. She swiftly ordered a fresh drink for Pierce and carried it over to the piano. With charm and persuasion, she convinced Pierce to find a seat.

Reluctantly, Pierce took the now-empty barstool beside Thad, his eyes still fixed on Billy. Viktoria joined Billy on the bench. She knew Pierce was trouble and was determined to keep him at bay.

Just then, a thunderous clamor rang out from the stairs. Billy turned toward the racket. It sounded like someone was trying to carry a large piece of furniture, maybe an overstuffed loveseat, way too big to make it up the narrow staircase, its sides scraping against the walls. Heads turned, and conversations halted as high heels clacking against the wooden steps echoed through the lounge. It was as if a marching band was parading up from the basement. The noise crescendoed until the door burst open with a final triumphant crash, revealing Misty Drizzle in all her dank and disheveled glory.

"Ladies and gentlemen, clear the runway! The queen has arrived!" Misty announced, her voice carrying over the hushed crowd. She stood in the doorway, her sequins catching the light and sending shimmering reflections across the room. Her grand entrance caught the attention of everyone in the room with a flourish of tarnished sequins and an air of judicial might. People grabbed hold of their drinks and steadied their tables as the five-foot-two tornado whirled through the tiny lounge, her presence like a force of nature. "Darling, I heard there was trouble, and where there's trouble, there's me!"

Billy rejoiced as if sighting the approaching cavalry to save the day.

Viktoria glanced over and saw Misty approaching. A sly smile crossed her lips. "Perfect timing, Misty. Thanks for responding to my S.O.S. We have a little situation here."

Misty smiled at Viktoria and maneuvered to Pierce like a small tank rolling steadily into battle. Pierce, distracted by

Misty's dramatic entrance and now proximity, looked for an escape route but was thwarted by her rapid-fire, animated conversation, which demanded all his attention and left him with no choice except to surrender.

With Pierce preoccupied, Viktoria returned to the piano and ended the set on a high note, belting out her last song, "When I Grow Too Old To Dream," casting a nostalgic spell across the room and calming the patrons.

The last call was announced, and the bar emptied, leaving only Billy, Viktoria, Thad, Pierce, the bartender, and Misty Drizzle. Pierce tried in vain to continue his shameless flirting with Thad over Misty's head, sneering at Billy as he did so.

In a bold move, Pierce broke free from his captor and suggested, "Thad, why don't we head over to the Sea Spray Inn for a nightcap?"

Billy was visibly uncomfortable with Pierce's advances toward Thad. Pierce was trying to wedge himself between them.

Then, as if on cue, Viktoria, the ever-concerned guardian angel, interceded on Billy's behalf. In a moment of clever distraction, she accidentally spilled her drink on Pierce.

"Hey! Look what you've done, you tacky bitch," Pierce snapped, jumping up.

"Oh, I'm so very sorry. Here, let me soak up some of that moisture," Viktoria responded, grabbing a handful of cocktail napkins and dabbing at the front of Pierce's soaked trousers.

Misty jumped up, ran to the bar for a towel, and pranced triumphantly to where Viktoria continued working on Pierce's lap. "Let me help, too. I want to dab at his crotch, too." Misty moved in on Pierce with the absorbent towel. Pierce batted at them in defense.

"Stop that. Get away from me, you—you freaks!" Pierce

roared, his face turning a deep shade of red. His eyes blazed with fury as he tried to push Viktoria and Misty away, his movements becoming more frantic and desperate.

"Calm down, darling," Viktoria said smoothly, still dabbing at his trousers. "We're just trying to help."

Pierce's frustration boiled over. "I don't need your help! This is ridiculous!" He shoved Viktoria's hand away, knocking the napkins to the floor. "You've ruined my night, you pathetic…"

Misty interrupted, her voice dripping with sarcasm. "Oh, honey, we're just getting started. Don't be such a drama queen."

That was the final straw for Pierce. With a furious snarl, he scrambled off the barstool, nearly tripping over his feet in haste. "I'm done with this place!" He sneered at Viktoria, then Misty, and finally turned his venomous gaze on Billy. "You can have your little circus. I'm out of here."

Pierce stormed out of La Péniche with one last look of contempt, the door slamming shut behind him with a resounding bang. The bar was silent momentarily, the air's tension palpable.

Billy couldn't help but smile at Viktoria and Misty's antics. They had given him the perfect opportunity. Billy hurriedly gathered the singles and a few fives from the tip jar and stuffed them into his front jeans pocket. He grabbed his backpack and slung it over one shoulder. His eyes darted across the dimly lit bar as he walked over to where Thad sat, nursing the last remnants of his scotch.

Billy noticed Thad's gaze was fixed on the near-empty glass before him. He looked like he was about to call it a night.

"Let's go for a walk."

The room seemed to grow still. Thad sighed, finally

looking up at Billy. "It's late, Billy, and you've been sitting there playing for hours; you must be dead tired."

He downed the rest of his scotch and stood. "I enjoyed meeting you, Billy, but my time at the shore is over. I've got to get back to Manhattan tomorrow." Even though Thad was curious to learn the real reason behind Billy's sudden departure from his job at the Sea Spray Inn, Thad didn't think this was the time or place to dig into that sensitive issue. And what would be the point? It was time to return to his life in Manhattan, get back to rehearsing with the Marsha Morgan Dance Company, and face reality. If he was feeling anything toward Billy, it was only a brief summer infatuation.

Billy's desperation heightened. He grabbed Thad's wrist to stop him. "I like to walk after playing. It helps me unwind. Walk with me. Please?"

Thad hesitated, torn between the three obvious reasons, at least to him, that prevented him from saying yes. Firstly, he was due to return to New York the next day and wanted to avoid getting entangled in a new relationship. Secondly, rehearsals for the dance company's upcoming season were set to begin in the next few weeks, and he still needed to get his hands on Emile Beauvais's new groundbreaking piece to complete the program. This latest work was earmarked for Mercer, Marsha Morgan's principal dancer. Marsha had even asked Liam to choreograph it, knowing that at her age, she needed to share her legacy with younger, more agile dancers and to preserve her place in history. Still, Emile was taking his sweet time finishing the piece. Marsha would be on his case when he returned to Manhattan if it wasn't delivered on time. Lastly, despite his fondness for Billy, he questioned whether Billy felt the same way about him. Nevertheless, Billy was captivating:

his smile, open manner, innocence, and the way he blushed—an attraction beyond their shared love for music.

Billy realized he was still holding Thad's wrist, and he released it, a faint blush coloring his cheeks. Thad recalled the endearing blush he had noticed during their first encounter by the stairs at the Sea Spray Inn. Their eyes met, and Thad's resistance slowly crumbled.

"All right, Billy, I'll walk with you for a while."

Viktoria and Misty clapped their hands, broad smiles beaming with approval. They said goodbye and began hustling the two men toward the stairs.

"Where to?" Thad asked.

"I'll show you. Come on."

Without waiting for further discussion, Billy bolted down the stairs, taking them two at a time, and headed toward the moonlit beach.

"Where are we going?"

"The boardwalk. It's great this time of night. You'll love it."

"But it's empty; nothing's open."

"That's why it's so great."

Billy led them down a side street that dead-ended at the Beachside boardwalk. A stretch of arcades, rides, and food stands slept in the semidarkness of mercury-vapor lamps and starlight. It was both eerie and beautiful.

They stepped onto the boards and walked south. Houses and hotels thinned out, replaced with dunes and seagrass. Billy took the flight of planked steps at the boardwalk's end down to the sand ten feet below. He disappeared under the boardwalk.

"I thought we were walking."

"We were, but now we're going to sit," Billy called up

from below. He popped out from under the boards, climbed up a few steps, reached for Thad's hand, hesitated, and said, "Follow me."

Billy slipped back under the boardwalk and cleared a spot with his feet. He scuffed away strands of dried seaweed and pieces of broken shells and plopped onto the sand, pulling Thad down beside him. When he reached for Thad's hand this time, he didn't hesitate. Thad's reflexes responded before his brain realized what was happening as his hand tightened around Billy's. He looked down at their clasped hands, blinked, and turned toward Billy, eyes wide, a frightened expression on his face.

"Hey, lean closer; I need to whisper a secret in your ear."

"You don't need to whisper, Billy. We're all alone; nobody can hear us anyway with the waves crashing like they are."

"You're no fun. So now, lean closer; this time, you have to shut your eyes, too."

Thad acquiesced, still tightly holding Billy's hand.

The kiss landed lightly on Thad's cheek. His eyes shot open, and Billy maneuvered his lips to Thad's mouth. And as tightly as he held onto the other man's hand, his lips followed suit, acting on their own, as the kiss deepened between them.

Billy's lips lingered on Thad's, the taste of salt and sea in the air adding a unique flavor to their kiss. The sound of the crashing waves served as a romantic backdrop to this unexpected moment of intimacy under the boardwalk.

As the kiss deepened, their bodies pressed closer together, and Thad's initial surprise gave way to a growing passion. His free hand found its way to the small of Billy's back, pulling him closer. The sensation of the cool sand beneath them contrasted with the heat building between them, making the moment feel all the more electrifying.

Moments passed like hours, and they finally broke the kiss, their foreheads resting against each other. Their breathing was heavy, and the world outside their little enclave seemed to disappear. Thad gazed into Billy's eyes, seeing both desire and uncertainty.

Billy's soft and sincere voice broke the silence. "Thad, I've wanted to do that for a long time."

Thad's smile deepened, and a rosy flush painted his cheeks as he gazed into Billy's eyes. "I've wanted it too, Billy. But..." Sensing the moment's gravity, Billy shifted slightly, still holding Thad's hand. "I want to tell you something," he began, his voice barely above a whisper. "I've always dreamed of composing a piece that captures the essence of everything I've ever felt—the joy, the pain, the love. Music has always been my way of making sense of the world, you know?"

Thad nodded, encouraging Billy to continue. "I get that. For me, it's always been about dance. Ever since I was a kid, I wanted to create something beautiful, something that would move people and make them feel alive. That's why I became a music director, to bring together the best of music and movement."

Billy's eyes sparkled with passion. "That's amazing. It's like we're both chasing the same dream in different ways. I want to write a symphony one day, something that will be remembered long after I'm gone. What about you, Thad? What's your ultimate dream?"

Thad took a deep breath, the sound of the waves providing a soothing backdrop. "My dream is to produce a full-scale production of an original ballet. Something that combines the elegance of classical dance with the raw energy of contemporary music. I'm no choreographer, but I have someone in mind who'd be perfect for the job: Liam Mercer. A performance that tells a story and evokes real emotions. And I want it to be perfect, something that can stand the test of time."

Billy smiled, squeezing Thad's hand. "I believe you can do it. You have the talent and the vision. Maybe one day, we can even collaborate on a project together. Can you imagine that?"

"I can, Billy. I really can. And I'd love nothing more than to see that happen. We must keep believing in and working toward our dreams, no matter what."

Billy nodded, determination filling his heart. "Yeah, no matter what. Thank you, Thad, for sharing this with me. It means a lot."

Thad smiled, leaning in for another kiss, this one filled with hope and the promise of a future where their dreams could intertwine. Billy leaned back slightly, his hand still intertwined with Thad's. "I never expected this," he admitted softly. "Meeting you, feeling this way…it's unexpected but wonderful."

Thad smiled, his thumb gently caressing the back of Billy's hand. "Life has a way of surprising us when we least expect it. Maybe this is exactly what we both needed."

Billy nodded, feeling a comforting sensation. "I've spent so much time focusing on my music and helping others that I forgot what it felt like to have someone truly see me."

Thad's gaze was steady, filled with understanding. "I see you, Billy. And I want to get to know you beyond the music and chaos. Just you."

Billy's heart swelled with emotion. "I'd like that too, Thad. Let's take it one step at a time and see where this leads."

Thad leaned in for another kiss, sealing the promise of their budding relationship.

Chapter 19

Beneath the boardwalk, the rhythmic pulse of the ocean waves bore witness to their secret meeting. Unable to resist the compelling force drawing him closer to Thad, Billy leaned in for another kiss, attempting to solidify the feelings that had been simmering beneath the surface, waiting to be revealed.

The kiss held promise, a tantalizing taste of what could be until Thad gently pulled back, their lips reluctantly parting. "But, Billy, hold on here." Thad's voice carried the weight of an impending departure. "As much as I'd like to pursue whatever is brewing between us, I leave for the city, my home, tomorrow. And you begin school in a few weeks; we can't do this."

Thad's words hung in the air as they stood in the shadow of the boardwalk. Despite the urge to explore what lay between them, time was running out. What began as a possible summer fling was now teetering on the edge of something more profound, yet moment by moment, Billy felt it slipping away.

"Don't say that," pleaded Billy, his eyes reflecting the starlight. "We're not that far apart, just a train ride. I'll come see you. I love New York."

Thad's gaze softened as if torn between the enchantment of the moment and the matter-of-fact reality of their separate lives. "We'll see, Billy. I think you're sweet, but we need to know more about each other before we pursue anything more serious."

As the moon spilled its silvery glow on the beach, rippling in sparkly eddies along the verge between incoming and outgoing waves, Thad stood, brushing off grains of sand and a few stray seaweed strands. He extended a hand to lift Billy, and together, they ascended the stairs to the boardwalk. The murmurs of the ocean served as a wistful soundtrack as the two men, bound by a nascent connection, faced their parting.

At the top of the stairs, Billy reached into his bag for a pen and something to write on. He found a piece of manuscript paper, tore off a corner, and scribbled his name and phone number on it. Handing it to Thad, he said, "Just in case."

Thad stuffed the scrap of paper deep into his jeans pocket but said nothing. Silence became their companion on the journey back, with Thad retracing his steps to the Sea Spray Inn and Billy pedaling home beneath the star-speckled sky. The night held promises and uncertainties, but for now, all that remained of their brief summer encounter was the taste of kisses and salt air on their lips.

Billy knew about love. He knew all too well about his unconditional love for Finn and how it manifested as companionship, loyalty, and protection. He also knew what it meant to love another human being: intimacy, romance, and emotional satisfaction. And he knew that both kinds of love involved passion, emotional intimacy, and shared experiences. The nature and complexity of love for a dog and intimate love for another person differed, but it somehow felt the same for him. He understood both, but as time went on after Finn's drowning, even now in his twenties, the second kind of love with another human, another man, was elusive. He'd had two brief relationships ending in difficult breakups, slammed doors, and unkind words. Whether he'd been taken advantage of by his lovers or feared loss down the road should a relationship die, he didn't want to deal with another heartbreak. He didn't want a broken heart incapable of healing, so he knew that if he tried to mend it and do it right, he'd have to persevere, overcome, and never give up. And yet, here was Thad, someone worth having a mended heart for.

As Billy pedaled home, he replayed the night's events in his mind. The way Thad had looked at him, the taste of his lips, the shared dreams whispered under the boardwalk—it all felt like the beginning of something significant. He didn't want to let it slip away.

Arriving at his apartment, Billy parked his bike and stood momentarily gazing up at the stars. He could barely make out the sound of waves rolling in at the beach, continuing their endless dance, and he felt peace wash over him. Whatever happened with Thad, he had to hold on to the hope and possibility that tonight had brought.

Inside, Billy washed up and tended to his injured hand. The makeshift bandage from the lifeguard had held up well, but he cleaned the wound carefully and applied a fresh bandage. He then sat at the piano, his fingers gently grazing the keys. Music had always been his refuge, his way of processing the world around him.

He played a soft, sad tune, letting the music flow from his heart. As the notes filled the room, he thought about the dreams he and Thad had shared. The idea of a collaboration between them was a beautiful vision that seemed almost too perfect to be real—but tonight had shown him that sometimes dreams could come true.

Billy's thoughts drifted back to Thad. The memory of

their kiss lingered, bringing a smile to his face. He wanted more than a fleeting summer romance. He wanted to explore his feelings and see where they might lead. It wouldn't be easy—Thad had his life in Manhattan, and Billy had his responsibilities here. Yet, it felt like both men were on the cusp of significant life changes.

As the final notes of his melody faded into the night, Billy made a silent vow. He would not let fear hold him back. He would reach out to Thad, visit him in New York, and see where it could lead. He was willing to take the risk, to open his heart again, and to pursue a love that felt worth fighting for.

Billy stood up from the piano and headed to bed, determined. The future was uncertain, but he knew that he had to try. For the first time in a long while, he felt hopeful about what lay ahead.

The following day, Saturday, Billy woke up with a renewed purpose. He picked up his phone to see if anyone—such as Thad—might have texted him or left a voicemail during the night. But no one had.

Billy spent the day preparing for the upcoming school year, practicing his piano pieces, and thinking about the possibilities ahead. The beach, the music, and the memory of Thad's kiss were all intertwined in his thoughts.

Later that evening at La Péniche, after the sun had set and the orange and pink twilight faded to an inky black, Billy's phone vibrated in the right back pocket of his jeans. He reached for it with his right hand, his left hand filling in with a clever moving bass line. There was a new message. His heart skipped a syncopated beat, but when he looked at the screen, it was just a notification about a software update.

Billy tried to brush off the growing unease. Maybe Thad

was busy. He reassured himself that Thad would contact him soon.

The next day came and went with no message from Thad. Billy's initial excitement began to wane. Doubts crept into his mind, and he started to second-guess what had happened under the boardwalk. Was Thad interested in him, or was their brief encounter just a diversion?

By the end of the week, the good feelings from that night had almost completely faded. Thad's silence gnawed at Billy, making him feel foolish for hoping for something more between them.

He wondered if he had misread everything: if Thad had just been polite, if the chaotic scene at La Péniche between the drag queens and Pierce had been too over-the-top, or if their dreams of collaboration were just fantasies. He realized he had to relinquish his expectations and move forward. If Thad did reach out, they could figure things out then. But for now, he had to focus on his own path, his music, and his dreams.

Chapter 20

"Thad, I need to speak with you immediately," Marsha's voice was sharp as she called him into her office.

Marsha's office was a cluttered haven of history and urgency, filled with the tangible echoes of a lifetime devoted to dance. The walls were adorned with framed posters from past productions, some yellowed with age, their edges curling like pages of old manuscripts. A large oak desk dominated the room, its surface buried under stacks of choreographic charts, production notes, and a teetering pile of unopened mail. The air was thick with the musty scent of old paper and the sharp, unsettling edge of worry.

The dim lighting, provided by a mismatched collection of lamps, cast shadows that danced eerily on the walls, adding to the atmosphere of controlled chaos. Marsha sat behind the desk, her posture rigid, as if held together by sheer willpower and the weight of her expectations. The room seemed to close in, the walls drawing tighter as Thad stepped in, every creak of the floorboards amplifying the silence that preceded her words.

Thad took a deep breath, bracing himself. He knew this conversation was inevitable. "Yes, Marsha?"

"Sit down." Marsha's tone brooked no argument. "Explain to me why we are less than a month away from opening night, and we still don't have a piece for Liam's solo. I promised him he'd have an opportunity to choreograph a new piece. We need to keep our talent engaged. I won't be around for too much longer. The company needs to go on without me, and we need young choreographers to create new work for the company to survive."

Thad sat, leaning forward with his elbows on his knees, his hands pressed against his forehead. "I... I trusted the composer, Marsha. He promised me he'd have it ready. I've been chasing him down, but he couldn't deliver."

Marsha's eyes, still piercing despite her age, narrowed. "You trusted him? Thad, this is not just about trust. It's about responsibility. You should have had a backup plan."

As Marsha spoke, her voice carried a critical edge sharp enough to cut through the mounting anxiety in the room. The air grew heavier with each word as if the atmosphere conspired to stifle Thad, squeezing the breath from his lungs. His palms were sweaty, leaving faint marks on the armrests of the wooden chair that felt uncomfortably small under the intense scrutiny of Marsha's gaze.

Thad sat up and faced his boss. "I know, Marsha. I know. And I'm sorry. But I'm working on it. I've contacted everyone I can think of to find a replacement."

"Sorry won't cut it, Thad," Marsha snapped. "Our company's reputation is at stake. Do you think our audience will care about your excuses? They expect excellence, and ensuring we deliver it is your job."

Thad clenched his fists, his patience wearing thin. "I'm doing everything I can! This was supposed to be a team effort. It's not like I wanted this to happen."

Marsha leaned forward, her expression softening slightly

but her voice still firm. "Thad, this is not about blame. It's about solutions. We need to figure this out, and we need to do it now."

Desperation crept into his voice. "Marsha, I need more time," he pleaded, his voice cracking.

Marsha didn't meet his eyes, her gaze fixed on the skyline visible through the office's narrow window. The evening light cast long shadows that made her seem more imposing. "Time isn't what we're short on, Thad. It's solutions," she said, her tone unwavering. The disappointment in her voice cut through the air, leaving a heavy silence in its wake.

"I've got a lead," Thad said, almost pleading. He had no one, but he wasn't about to share that information with Marsha. He'd try one more time to reach out to a few composers who might be able to come up with something on the spur of the moment, but he didn't want to make any more promises, especially to Marsha. "I'll take care of it."

Marsha's expression softened further, showing a rare glimpse of the mentor beneath the tough exterior. "I know you will, Thad. Just remember, the company is counting on you."

Thad nodded, the gravity of the situation settling over him like a heavy mantle. "I'll do it, Marsha. I'll make it right."

Thad left Marsha's office, her final words about the company's reliance on him echoing in his mind as a constant reminder of the high stakes involved—his failure could jeopardize the company's future. Despite the sprig of lavender on her desk, which was meant to be calming, it did nothing to soothe his growing anxiety. He knew what he had to do.

On his way out, he bumped into Liam, who was still working with several other dancers. Thad paused to watch and was reminded of Liam's total commitment to the company and his fellow dancers. Thad couldn't let him down. He needed to hurry home and handle this crisis.

As he walked through the park, Thad's thoughts wandered. Fallen leaves and brittle twigs crumbled and snapped under his feet, leaving a wake of autumn's discards behind him. His mind drifted back to his first meeting with Marsha ten years ago. He recalled the sunny afternoon, the famous choreographer's firm handshake despite her gnarled, arthritic fingers, and his naive optimism that once brimmed with limitless possibility—until today.

Then, without warning, Billy's face flashed in his mind. He remembered how Billy's eyes lit up when he talked about music, the passion in his voice, and the softness of his kiss under the boardwalk. The memory was both a comfort and a torment. It seemed that whenever Thad found himself alone with his thoughts, Billy crept in, uninvited but not unwelcome. He couldn't help but wonder if he had made a mistake by pushing Billy away.

Thad tried to shake off the distraction. He had a job to do, and personal regrets had no place here. But as he continued through the park, the image of Billy lingered, casting a shadow over his thoughts about the upcoming dance season.

He continued to Columbus Circle, descending into the city's underbelly at Fifty-Ninth Street and joining the constant flux of characters on the Broadway-Seventh Avenue Local, the Downtown 1 train. The ride was a blur, punctuated by the jostling chaos of the city's eclectic jumble of commuters. The stale air of the subway tinged with the acrid stench of urine and the metallic tang of heated steel, made his stomach churn. Food vendors' faint but pervasive scent lingered, mixing uncomfortably with the odor of bodies after a full day's work packed tightly together. At the Christopher Street-Sheridan Square station, he left the melee, but not before enduring an indecent pat-down from a pervy turnstile, climbed to the surface, and headed to his apartment on Barrow Street. The familiarity of his neighborhood brought no comfort; the unresolved crisis clung to him, its tension tightening around him as he entered his home. The fresh air above ground did little to cleanse his senses, leaving a sour aftertaste of the subway's oppressive atmosphere in his mouth.

Thad lived in a quaint garden-level unit in the heart of the West Village. The classic brownstone facade was trimmed with intricate wrought-iron railings, cascading flower boxes, and the blackened parasitic tendrils of fire escapes long attached to its host. Inside, hardwood floors and exposed brick led to smooth plaster walls showcasing carefully lit artwork. A grand piano dominated the living room, which flowed into a spacious dining area and a well-sized kitchen by New York standards.

The main bedroom, nestled at the back, offered a serene retreat. French doors from the living room and bedroom opened to a private courtyard. The meticulously manicured space, frequented by squirrels, birds, and butterflies, gave Thad a green oasis amid Manhattan's dense cityscape.

Thad placed his portfolio on the sofa, started a fresh pot of coffee, and began rifling through every contact that might magically help him conjure up a lead. He scrolled through his contacts, rummaged through a pile of unfiled paperwork, and checked old Playbills for musicians he had worked with during past seasons. He called whoever might hold promise. A few were interested but had nothing ready; all were sympathetic, but in the end, no one came forward with a solution to Thad's dilemma.

He had been at it for hours, hitting walls and dead ends, and desperately needed to clear his head. He poured himself a bourbon and sat down at the piano, his go-to sanctuary for relaxation. Playing had always been his way to unwind. He started with Bach's French Suite No. 2 in C Minor, a piece he knew by heart. Despite its flawless execution, it did little to soothe his restless mind. He needed a change.

He reached for a book of show tunes and standards he kept for impromptu sing-alongs. He placed the book, spine down, on the piano's top and let it fall open to a random page. The front and back covers made a soft thud, and the pages spread open like the wings of an uchiwa fan, revealing a cascade of melodies as if in a flip-book animation. At this point, he didn't care which song appeared. He just wanted something, anything, to play and shift his mood.

The book opened to "I Fall In Love Too Easily." At first, Thad wasn't familiar with it; he thought it was some old tune from an obscure musical from the 1940s. But as soon as he finished the first eight bars, he remembered Billy Pine accompanying a woman at La Péniche. It was this song. When he finished playing it, the answer to his missing dance piece revealed itself. Billy's composition would be perfect for Liam's solo. However, this solution came with a new dilemma.

On the one hand, Billy's composition would be perfect for Liam's solo. Conversely, would Billy even be willing to share that haunting piece? Would Billy even be interested in hearing from him after months of silence, the silence he brought on while trying to put distance between them when he realized he had real feelings for him? There was only one way to find out. All he had to do was find that scrap of paper with Billy's phone number.

Chapter 21

Today was Viktoria's day to read to prisoners, leaving Misty Drizzle to manage their drag accessory shop, The Flambroidery. After a hellish morning cleaning up the mess her cat, Bellicose, had made by throwing up on her vision board, Viktoria Sinclair sat at her vanity, surrounded by an eclectic array of makeup products. The legend of Le Péniche was about to perform a transformation that would leave everyone in awe, even herself. At nearly sixty, Viktoria's face, which one might say was built for rock climbing with its vertical and horizontal geometry, was her canvas. Applying makeup to it was like manipulating a technicolor Etch A Sketch, where every stroke had to move in straight lines.

She looked into the mirror, her steely eyes scrutinizing every pore. "Well, darling, let's get to work," she murmured to her reflection, reaching for the industrial-strength spackle—her full-coverage foundation. She applied a thick layer with a surgeon's precision and an artist's flair, erasing any sign of natural skin tone.

"Contouring is an art form, and this face is my Sistene Chapel," she mused aloud, enjoying the solitary ritual. Viktoria grabbed her concealer, several shades lighter than her foundation, and began highlighting. She carefully applied the product under her eyes, along the bridge of her nose, and on her chin. The transformation was taking shape, and she could already see the glow emerging.

Next came the contouring. Viktoria picked up a contour stick dramatically darker than her skin tone and carved out cheekbones that could cut glass. "If these cheekbones were any sharper, they'd be classified as weapons," she joked to herself, a wry smile on her lips.

With her face now a complex map of light and shadow, Viktoria reached for her beauty sponge and began blending. "Blend, blend, blend," she chanted like a mantra, "because harsh lines are for amateurs." She moved the sponge with skill and expertise, softening the edges into a seamless gradient.

Satisfied with her blending, Viktoria set her masterpiece with a generous dusting of translucent powder. "This face isn't going anywhere," she declared to her reflection, patting the powder into place. "Not even if I sweat enough to fill a kiddie pool."

With the contouring complete, she moved on to the finishing touches: bold eye makeup, false lashes that could double as whisk brooms, and perfectly sculpted eyebrows that would make even the most seasoned makeup artists envious. Finally, she applied her signature deep red lipstick, adding the last touch of drama.

As she donned her wig—a voluminous cascade of curls—and slipped into a dazzling costume, Viktoria admired her reflection. "How do I look?" she asked, posing and winking at her image in the mirror.

The answer was clear: she looked every bit the drag legend she was, ready to conquer the world, even if it was just her living room. With a deep breath and a final check in the mirror, Viktoria Sinclair embraced the fierce, fabulous, and utterly unforgettable persona she had perfected over decades.

"Showtime," she whispered to herself. With a confident smile, she stepped out of her vanity space, grabbed her keys and props, and left her apartment just above The Flambroidery. She got into her car and headed for the prison.

She went through security at the main gate, presented her ID—which bore an image that looked nothing like the woman behind the steering wheel and a name, Victor Schumann, that didn't match—smiled at the guard, and found a parking spot near the entrance. She checked her makeup one last time in the visor mirror. Once through a second tier of security, she strutted down the dimly lit Coastal State Correctional Facility corridors. She didn't need to make a grand entrance because no one was roaming the secured prison hallways. Most inmates and guards were safely tucked away in cell blocks or completing lunch shifts in the cafeteria. Others were on various work details or out exercising in the yard. But cameras documented her long walk to the library, and she would give them a show if anyone were watching. Her heels clicked against the cold concrete floor. She was no stranger to performing, but this stage was unlike any she had ever graced. Gone were the dazzling lights of the drag clubs and the adoring applause of her loyal fans at Le Péniche. In their place stood rows of barred cells and the curious gazes of hardened criminals.

At fifty-seven, Viktoria was a legend in the drag community, known for her impeccable style, quick wit, and heart of gold. But age had taken its toll, and her once flamboyant costumes were now replaced with more subdued ensembles tailored to accommodate her aging body and income. Yet, despite the wrinkles that lined her face and the gray streaks that peppered her hair, there was still a sparkle in her eye and a fire in her soul.

Viktoria had been volunteering at the prison, hosting a weekly reading hour for the inmates. It was her way of giving back to the community that had embraced her when she was just a young drag queen trying to find her place in the world. She had been a regular member of the Book Jacket Sisterhood, a rag-tag group of queens who read to children at the Beachside Public Library. The group's name originated when one of its members began applying rhinestones and glitter to add a bit of glamour to the covers of the books they read to their adoring young fans. It was fun until one Saturday morning when the Sisterhood approached the library for a ten o'clock reading, only to be barred from entering the building by a small but mean-spirited group of protesting citizens. The mayor, facing reelection and running on a "restore decency" platform, immediately called for the end of drag queen story hour. While the Sisterhood and its allies continued to protest the mayor's decision, Viktoria decided to take her business elsewhere and found an unlikely sanctuary at the state prison, where no morality police on the outside cared what happened within the correctional institution's walls.

As Viktoria navigated the labyrinth of corridors and tunnels to the library, she reflected on why she had come alone this time. Last time, she had brought Misty Drizzle to read to the inmates. Unfortunately, Misty's enormous hoop skirt had raised security concerns, mainly when they tried to leave the prison. The guards thought she might be attempting to smuggle out a convict or two. Things escalated when Misty gave the guards a hard time, leading to an invasive full-body strip search and the rather undignified use of her legal name, Mitchell Driscoll. After that unfortunate spectacle, it was decided that Misty would stay behind to run The Flambroidery during future prison visits—a role she appreciated far more than being thoroughly searched for possible escapees.

As Viktoria approached the library, she observed the gathering: a diverse mix of men, each absorbed in books or card games. Her incarcerated boyfriend, Wally, was there, too. Upon her entrance, heads turned, some curious, others indifferent. Undeterred, Viktoria offered a composed smile before addressing the group.

"Good afternoon, darlings! Are you ready to be educated, inspired, and entertained?" Viktoria took command of the room, her voice ringing out with a theatrical flourish. "It's time for another fabulous reading hour with yours truly, Viktoria Sinclair! Today, I thought we'd dive into the world of classic literature," she declared, holding up a weathered copy of *Pride and Prejudice*. "Who's up for a little Jane Austen?"

As Viktoria launched into her reading, her voice filled the room, transporting the inmates to a world far removed from the confines of their cells and oppressive monotony. For the next hour, she regaled them with tales of love, scandal, and societal intrigue, her melodious voice weaving a spellbinding tapestry of words.

Amidst the laughter and applause, Viktoria caught Wally's eye. He gestured that he wanted to talk after the session. His piercing slate eyes and rugged good looks set him apart. There was an air of mystery about him, a hint of sadness that tugged at Viktoria's heartstrings, and she couldn't wait to hear what he had to say.

As the reading hour drew to a close, Viktoria went over to where Wally sat; a guard joined her for protection when the two began to talk. She thought he seemed nervous, perhaps more like excited anticipation.

"Hiya, Vik. I've got the best news. I'm being paroled next month. What do you think of that?"

Viktoria beamed and nearly embraced Wally when the guard stepped between them, enforcing the no-touching rule between visitors and prisoners. Viktoria took two steps backward, raising her hands as if nothing had happened.

"Oh, Wally, that is the best news I've gotten in weeks. Why are you getting out early?"

Wally lowered his head, circling the ball of his right foot on the polished cement floor. When he looked up into Viktoria's eyes, she thought he might even say, "Aw, shucks, ma'am," like some bashful cowboy, but all he said was, "Good behavior, Vik, for you."

Viktoria's heart soared as the guard led Wally back to his cell. As she packed up her belongings and bid Wally farewell, she couldn't help but reflect on his journey.

She remembered first meeting him during one of her volunteer visits. Despite his rough exterior, Wally showed genuine eagerness to turn his life around. He had shared with her stories of his troubled past, growing up in a struggling family on the outskirts of Beachside and falling in with the wrong crowd during his teenage years. His natural talent for mechanics had always been overshadowed by his poor decisions, culminating in the robbery attempt that landed him in prison.

Yet, during his time in prison, Wally had worked hard to change. He had earned his GED and participated in vocational training, focusing on mechanics. Viktoria had witnessed his transformation, and seen his determination to leave his past mistakes behind and build a better future.

"Remember, Wally," Viktoria called out, her voice

echoing slightly in the large room, "you've got a real talent. Use it. Make something of yourself."

Wally turned back, his eyes shining with gratitude and determination. "I will, Vik. I promise."

As Viktoria left the prison, she wondered what the future held for Wally. She hoped he would find the stability and success he longed for, perhaps even opening his own garage someday. She knew his journey wouldn't be easy, but she believed in him. After all, he had shown incredible strength and resilience, qualities that would serve him well in the outside world.

Back in her car, Viktoria took a moment to collect her thoughts. The stark contrast between her glamorous world of drag and the harsh realities of the prison never ceased to amaze her. But in these moments of contrast, she felt most alive, most connected to the human experience.

Driving towards Beachside to join Billy for dinner, she was eager to fill him in about Wally. Billy had always been her rock, someone who understood the ups and downs of her life without judgment. She knew that Billy, with his kind heart and generous spirit, would be just as thrilled about Wally's impending release.

"Maybe Billy can help me figure out a plan for Wally," she mused aloud, the idea comforting her. "He always has such good advice."

With a final glance at the prison in her rearview mirror, Viktoria refocused on the road ahead. Tonight, she would find solace in the company of a dear friend, and together, they would celebrate small victories and plot a course for brighter days. The future might be uncertain, but with friends like Billy, she wouldn't have to face it alone.

Chapter 22

Billy dashed up the side stairs to his apartment on Maple Avenue, a simple one-bedroom affair above an old carriage house hidden behind a charming yet substantial cedar-shake house that was once the gatehouse to a sprawling estate long since parceled off for building lots. The two structures were all that remained of the property, the main house having been torn down more than fifty years ago; its ornate fountains and sculptures replaced with children's playgrounds and a community swim club, all to make room for middle-class families. His apartment was just a few blocks from his father's house, where Maple ended, forming a "T" intersection with River Road. He threw his backpack in the corner next to his piano and rushed into the kitchen to see what he could muster for supper. Viktoria was due any minute, and his school chorus practice had run late. Then, before he could get out of the building, the principal had asked to speak with him about dates for the school's winter and spring concerts, making sure to avoid vacations and testing days, which kept him delayed even longer. There was no time to stop for groceries, so he'd have to make do with leftovers. He hoped Viktoria could deal with that.

No sooner had he pulled various Tupperware containers of half-eaten meals from the fridge than there was a knock on the door. Billy checked his watch as he crossed the room to answer the door; it was nearly six o'clock.

Viktoria crossed the threshold with a vitality that bordered on flamboyance in a seductive green velour jumpsuit with frilly cuffs and pant legs as if someone had playfully trimmed the excess off a feathered boa and fastened the remnant frills to her wrists and ankles. It seemed a bit much, Billy pondered, for a school night. She offered one cheek for an air kiss and then the other. Billy then went in for a hug.

Despite rushing around to find suitable fare for the evening's meal, Billy had set a bottle of red wine and two glasses on the coffee table.

"Wine?"

"Oh, please, do you even have to ask? I'd love a glass." Before Billy could get to the table to do the honors, Viktoria unscrewed the cap and poured herself a large glass of wine. She turned toward Billy, "Want some?" and dispensed an equally full serving for him.

He two sat down on the loveseat. Viktoria gazed at the kitchen area and let her nose direct her head in a spastic circling motion from side to side as if she were sniffing for something—a rabbit, squirrel, or a missing child—anything that might be simmering on the stove.

"I normally would commend you for the usual lovely aroma wafting from your kitchen heralding our anticipated meal—you're an excellent cook, Billy—but I smell nothing. Nothing!"

"Sorry, Viktoria, I got held up at school and didn't have time to stop for something for tonight's meal. I have a few leftovers I could cobble together to make a—"

Viktoria's hand palmed to Billy's face as if she were about to lipsync to a classic Supreme hit. "Stop in the name of...

food. But I have the most incredible news before we decide on dinner."

Billy raised an eyebrow, intrigued. "Oh? Do tell."

Viktoria took a deep breath, her eyes shining with excitement. "Wally's getting out of prison next month!"

Billy's eyes widened in surprise, then lit up with delight. "Oh my goodness, Vik, that's incredible! How did that happen?"

"Good behavior," Viktoria said, her voice trembling slightly with emotion. "He's been such a model inmate, and it's all because he wanted to make me proud. I'm the rehabilitation messiah!"

Billy reached over and took Viktoria's hand, squeezing it reassuringly. "You must be over the moon. What are you going to do to celebrate?"

Viktoria laughed a little shakily. "I haven't even had time to think about it yet. I was so excited to tell you."

Billy leaned back, his expression thoughtful. "Well, we'll have to plan something special for his homecoming. He will need all the support he can get to reintegrate into the outside world."

"You're right," Viktoria agreed, her mind racing with ideas. "He's been through so much. I want to ensure he knows he has a place and people who care about him."

Billy raised his glass in a toast. "To Wally's new beginning and the wonderful life you'll help him build."

Viktoria clinked her glass against Billy's, her eyes shining with hope. "To new beginnings," she echoed.

They sipped their wine in comfortable silence, both lost in their thoughts about the future. Viktoria felt a renewed purpose. She had always believed in the transformative power of love and community, and now she had a chance to put those beliefs into action.

"So," Billy said, breaking the silence, "what's the first step? Have you thought about where he'll stay or what he'll do?"

"I'm not sure yet," Viktoria admitted. "But I want him to stay with me in my extra bedroom until he gets back on his feet and finds his own place. Unless, of course, something more serious develops between us, and he moves into my bedroom with me. He'll need stability and support."

Billy nodded approvingly. "That sounds like a great plan. And I'll be here to help with anything you need."

"Thank you, Billy. You've always been my rock," Viktoria said, her voice filled with gratitude.

Billy waved her thanks away with a smile. "We're family, Vik. We take care of each other."

As they continued to discuss their plans for Wally's release, excitement and determination welled up in Viktoria. With Billy by her side, she knew they could help Wally successfully transition back into the world. The future was uncertain, but they could face anything together with love and support.

"Let's celebrate tonight. How about Carmine's?"

Billy grinned. "That sounds perfect. Let me grab my coat."

Most of the restaurants in Beachside had closed for the season, and all the boardwalk joints and arcades were boarded up for protection against Nor'easters' devastating wind, sleet, and rain. Still, a few establishments with solid local followings remained open all winter. And Carmine's had a wood-burning fireplace to ward off the seasonal chill. It was cozy, too, with checkered oilcloth-draped tables and murals of lava-spewing volcanoes and quaint hilltop towns providing a false Italian narrative on the walls. It had a Jersey vibe. If you were in the mood for something fancier, you could drive over to Ocean Point for what was considered by the more well-off as fine dining with exorbitantly high prices.

They were seated at a table by the fire, Viktoria's green outfit clashing in jittery contrast to the red checks on the tablecloth like an animated optical hallucination. They ordered a tomato pie and a bottle of red.

"Billy, dearest, how is school going? Do you love your kiddos?"

"School's great! The kids are great, but it's still early in the year. Give it time for their true colors to shine. I have a wonderful group of fourth graders who can sing, which makes the class enjoyable for them and me."

Billy chomped down on a slice of pizza as Viktoria changed the subject.

"Have you heard from that wonderful man, the musical director with the New York dance company...now what was his name?"

Billy tinkered with his cutlery as the question left Vik's mouth. "You know full well what his name is, Vik. Thad."

"Yes, that dreamboat. Thad. Have you heard from him?"

"No, I haven't. Not since he left. I guess it wasn't meant to be. I liked him and thought there was something between us. But he's in the city, and with all the shenanigans involving Pierce, he might have thought anything between us would be too messy."

"Don't do that. Stop clinking your silverware." Billy stopped fidgeting and crossed his arms over his chest.

"And don't do that, Billy—talk yourself out of something that might be a promising relationship. It was clear to me, anyway, that he was into you. His eyes were all over you. A bit cruisey, but in a good way."

Billy remembered the kiss they shared just two blocks from Carmine's that night under the boardwalk. The last time he saw Thad.

"I don't know, but there was something there that doesn't just go away when summer ends and the world gets back to business. You should give him a call."

"I don't have his number. And don't tell me to look him up online. He made it clear that he didn't have time for a relationship, let alone a friendship, with me. But I do think about him all the time."

"Well, maybe his dance company will have a performance this fall. We could get tickets to one of the shows, and you could surprise him. What do you think about that?"

"In a perfect world? Maybe. But I don't want to interfere with his life—I mean work. It's a nice thought, though."

"Maybe I'll buy tickets for your birthday, and we can make a day of it in the city."

"My birthday's in January, Vik, which you know darn well."

"Well, maybe I'll buy tickets for someone with a birthday this fall, not tell them, and take you instead."

"I don't know. I'd like to see him and attend one of his performances, but I don't know."

"Oh, and we could go to that charming little restaurant you like so much on Restaurant Row, um, Curtain Call. Wouldn't that be fun?"

The mention of the restaurant's name took Billy back

to the first time he went there after a matinee performance. He remembered how the soft lights in the small dining room illuminated walls adorned with nostalgic show posters and Playbills, transporting guests back to the bygone glamour of Broadway's golden age. He'd returned many times since, especially after seeing a show or visiting a museum.

Viktoria noticed Billy's distant gaze. "Yoo-hoo, Billy dear, you seem to have spaced out. Where'd you go?"

"Oh, sorry, Vik. Just thinking about that restaurant gives me a good feeling. I'm back now."

Billy and Viktoria sat quietly, chatting and finishing their supper, enjoying their time together and the radiating heat from the fireplace. They left Carmine's, and Viktoria dropped Billy off at his driveway, catapulting wildly gestured air kisses his way as she sped off.

Once inside, Billy grabbed his lesson plan book and headed to bed to tweak a couple of lessons for tomorrow's classes. At least, that was his intention. His phone rang. It was late. Had something happened at home? Was his dad okay?

Chapter 23

"Hello?"

"Billy, how are you doing?"

Billy's breath caught in his throat; his tongue suffered temporary paralysis, unable to utter a response.

"Hello? Billy?"

Once his airway cleared and he could swallow, he answered. "Thad, how are you? It's been months."

"Funny how time does that." Here's where Thad ended the niceties and got down to business. "Billy, listen, I've got a huge favor to ask, and I hope you can do it."

Billy sensed this wasn't a call to catch up on the time since they separated from that tender kiss under the boardwalk in the summer. If he had to name Thad's tone, it was impatient and lacking warmth, like a bottom-line business call.

Thad laid out his problem step by step, more to make sense of what had happened with the temperamental composer than to explain to Billy exactly what favor he needed.

"Emile Beauvais, the composer I commissioned for a new work for the dance company, backed out at the last moment, which pissed me off since we needed his composition to round out the program. Our fall season is nearly sold out, and I don't have a replacement, not even one of my own, to take its place. Marsha's beside herself, and now it's all on me. I have to handle it."

"I'm sorry, Thad. Don't you have a composition from another season that you could use for that spot?"

"Uh-uh. The two that might work require the entire company. We've got a few new dancers joining the troupe, and having them learn the choreography at this late date is too much to ask. Besides, they're too lengthy for the program as it now stands. I need a solo piece for Liam Mercer, our principal dancer. Marsha wants him to choreograph it, something new, rather than try to resurrect a piece from the repertoire."

"Thad, I'd like to help, but I'm unsure what you're calling me for."

"Remember that piece you played for me at the Sea Spray Inn? Did you ever finish it?"

Billy remembered the piece. He couldn't forget it. The piece was linked to a sorrow he knew he'd carry with him for the rest of his life.

"Yes, I finished it." Billy's heart picked up its tempo, and something anticipatory took flight, hovering between hope and fear. "It took me a while to nail down the coda, but when I did, it felt right. It's not long, about seven minutes. Other than that, it's the same piece I played for you before. I'm titling it 'Transcendence.'"

"Perfect! That's about the same length as the one we've had to go without."

Billy waited, hesitating to ask the question he knew Thad was about to ask.

"Billy, I'd like you to send me a recording. You don't have to go to a studio to record it; use your phone. I want Marsha to listen to it."

"I can do that, but why?"

"If Marsha agrees, we'd like to include it in our upcoming season. Liam Mercer will choreograph and dance it as a solo—just him. I believe his choreographic skills can match the intensity of your music."

Billy nearly fell out of bed. "Wow! I don't know what to say. Okay, I'll do it. I'll make the recording tomorrow at school. The piano there is in better tune and sounds better than mine at home. I'll get it to you tomorrow."

"That's wonderful. You saved me."

Billy considered the *you-saved-me*. He'd heard it before, and it ended in a kitchen disaster. He wondered when someone might save him.

Now that the reason for the call had been addressed and Thad had gotten what he needed, Billy wanted to get personal. "I've missed you." But before he could continue, Thad interrupted.

"Sorry, Billy, another time. I have to go. Talk soon, and I'll let you know what Marsha decides."

The phone went dead. So much for being saved tonight.

Chapter 24

Billy frequently took the train into Manhattan after Marsha agreed to include his piece in the upcoming season. Sometimes, he rode the bus or drove himself, parking at the Port Authority Bus Terminal. Balancing his school job with rehearsals in the city was madness, but he managed it well and enjoyed being in the city and having his music appreciated. His crosstown trek to the Marsha Morgan Dance Company's studios on East 63rd Street soon became a habit, like a daily commute.

On his first trip, Billy boarded the Uptown 1 at Penn Station, heading toward the dance studio on East 63rd Street. As the train rumbled toward 42nd Street-Times Square, Billy settled into the bustling atmosphere and couldn't help but notice three riders dressed in oversized, fleece-covered, reticulated foam vegetable costumes. A giant carrot and a broccoli spear were squeezed into the narrow seats, drawing amused glances from other passengers. Next to them stood a third character, a peapod. The front of the peapod looked as if it had been unzipped, revealing six large peas protruding like a vertical set of exposed breasts. The sight was both comical and slightly outrageous but mostly just plain indecent.

Unable to find a seat, Billy ended up standing beside the peapod. He grabbed the vertical pole nearby for balance as the train swayed and jolted along the tracks. The peapod, noticing Billy's struggle to stay upright, playfully offered, "Hold onto my pod if you need to steady yourself!" The peapod then gave its exposed peas a suggestive jiggle, winking at Billy with a flourish as hilariously inappropriate as it was absurd.

Billy couldn't suppress his laughter. "What's the occasion?" he asked, his curiosity in full operational mode.

The carrot, whose face barely peeked out from the top of the costume, wore a green felt beanie secured under its chin by an elastic cord adorned with spiky fake stems that sprouted from the top of its head. The carrot's gender was challenging to determine beneath the concealing costume. It turned to him and said, "We're headed to a school assembly on nutrition. Gotta teach the kids to eat their veggies!"

The broccoli, also of indeterminate gender, nodded enthusiastically, the costume's fake florets bouncing. "It's a tough job, but someone's got to do it!"

The peapod, noticing Billy's bemused expression, added, "And I'm here to ensure they eat their peas, too! I know my look is a little risqué for a peapod, but you've gotta catch their attention somehow, right?"

Billy grinned as he tightened his grip on the pole for another bump in the track. "Well, you're making a memorable impression. Good luck!"

As the train approached 42nd Street-Times Square, the carrot attempted to stand, but the sudden jerk of the train caused it to topple over, bumping into the broccoli, which in turn fell against the peapod. Billy reflexively tightened his hold on the pole to steady himself while the vegetable trio ended up in a tangled heap on the floor. The peapod's costume burst open further, revealing even more of the large, exposed peas.

Watching the vegetable medley struggle to get back on their feet brought an unexpected moment of amusement to Billy's busy day. A few passengers laughed, some gasped, and one yelled, "Where's the Green Giant when you need him?" The carrot, quick on its feet, retorted, "He's already at the school setting up for the program." Most riders returned to their books and phones, barely blinking at the strange spectacle.

At the 42nd Street-Times Square station, Billy bid the vegetable trio goodbye and exited the train. He navigated the sea of people and flashing lights to the 42nd Street-Bryant Park station, where he hopped on the Q train to the Upper East Side.

Billy arrived at the Lexington Avenue-63rd Street station with a lighter heart, the vegetable caper still fresh in his mind. His pace quickened as he neared the dance studio; excitement and anticipation buzzed within him, and he was ready to embrace the opportunities ahead.

Bare-chested and wearing tights, Liam Mercer met Billy at the studio's main entrance and escorted him upstairs. Following Liam up the stairs, Billy appreciated Liam's perfect form, sheening in a thin layer of sweat as if he'd just finished an intense workout.

There was no wasted energy in his movement. Every step was deliberate as if it had been choreographed. Billy could tell Liam's body was a perfect storm of strength, flexibility, and agility. He was well-proportioned and toned, emphasizing an aesthetic definition without excessive bulk. His powerful legs and slender waist allowed for a wide range of movement.

Billy saw how his body had one purpose: to support the demands of intricate and expressive choreography. His well-defined abdominal muscles let Billy know he'd have the stamina to control movements and maintain balance for extended periods.

Liam led him to a large, second-floor dance studio with windows looking down onto a small courtyard and out onto the street. The Upper Eastside was reflected in the floor-to-ceiling mirrors on the opposite wall—a handful of folding chairs and a massive concert grand stood by the windows.

The first time Billy sat at the piano, the notes he produced seemed drowned out by the sheer strength and beauty of the dancer, as if the sounds had nowhere to go. Liam's athleticism and power shattered the music, leaving Billy's carefully constructed opus plastered against the windows, walls, and mirrors, with no escape. He hadn't seen this much flesh on one person since last summer at the beach. But unlike Beachside, where bodies ranged from obese to skeletal, the body before him was perfect.

Thad let Billy dither away at the piano until the dance sequence seemed to come apart at the seams. Liam haphazardly spiraled to the floor as he looked at Billy and then at Thad, both men's faces blank and emotionless. Billy quickly realized that Thad wasn't the only director in the room. A dancer had just schooled him. But Liam began to smile, not in sympathy but in support, when Billy realized he'd fallen short, a teachable moment for sure. Billy could do better.

"You're breathing like a musician, a singer, and that won't work here." Thad gestured toward Liam. "You need to breathe like a dancer. Watch."

Thad signaled to Liam to repeat part of the opening sequence. Billy focused on the dancer's breath, the space and time his breath would cover, and his movement riding on top of it to its completion. He noticed a discernible sharp tensing of his body with each inhale, followed by an opposite and clear release with each exhale. He could understand that physicalizing of body and breath as a musician, the purposeful building of tension, whether melodic, harmonic, or rhythmic, in a musical phrase, section, or scattered throughout an entire work, that always called for release, for resolution. It was an interdisciplinary awakening for him: seeing and acknowledging the commonality between two art forms: the one that he knew, music, and the one that he now saw before him in the dancer.

Billy had attended dance performances when the American Ballet Theatre or New York City Ballet were in residence at Lincoln Center. He was always impressed with how dancers seemed to defy gravity, how they launched themselves into midair effortlessly, and how they could pause as if suspended in time feet above the stage: elevation and ballon.

With modern dance, it was different; ballet had an inherent gracefulness, refined and elegant, lyrical and delicate. Morgan's technique, like Martha Graham's, expressed a severity and weightiness that understood the human condition through the force of gravity—like the weight he felt when Finn was trapped under the ice, a weight that always seemed to be present—the constant contractions and releases and spiraling through the pelvis and torso, falling and rising and falling again.

Billy saw how Liam exhibited a broader range of muscle development, emphasizing overall strength and flexibility that allowed a greater range of motion rather than a ballet dancer's lean, elegant, and elongated muscles. His body was better suited to executing fluid and dynamic movements characteristic of modern dance.

Billy also noticed that Liam danced barefoot; no pointe

shoes or ballet slippers protected his feet. His feet looked like they'd just lost a street fight: calluses, bruises, blisters, and a wide range of toe deformities. Liam's feet were beaten up, a testament to his dedication and the physicality of his art form and a complete contrast to his otherwise physical perfection.

Billy noticed something else while seated at the piano watching the dancer move, something he intuited as a child and grew to deeply understand as he got older, especially while studying music at college. Now, he saw it come to life right before him. Music, when performed, existed in time: the duration of sounds, silences, tempos, and dynamics that spanned seconds and minutes or hours. Dance, however, lived in both space and time. It was different. At that moment, he considered that duality as one, something more complete, a perfect art form.

"Let's try this again," Thad told him. "But this time, I want you to be more deliberate in your playing. Connect with the dancer and mean it."

As Thad approached Billy quietly from behind, Liam scrambled off the floor and took his position. His hands found Billy's shoulders, applying just enough pressure to convey a presence without disrupting Billy's focus. Still, a shiver ran down his spine. He was keenly aware of Thad's cologne, that wonderful woodsy scent spiked with a hint of cinnamon that he had first encountered at the Sea Spray Inn. How could he keep his mind on the task at hand? Why was he standing so close? What was he doing with his hands?

Thad counted off the tempo. Billy's senses awakened in response; his every nerve attuned to the rhythm as it pulsed through him. Billy caught the upbeat with a dissonant glissando, but it was the downbeat that ignited a newfound fervor within him, a surge of energy that he had never experienced before. Thad's touch became more deliberate as he played, subtly guiding Billy. With each phrase, the pressure on his shoulders shifted, mimicking the rise and fall of the music and syncing with Liam's breath.

With each crescendo, Thad's silent urging propelled Billy to new heights of aesthetic passion, his fingers dancing across the keys with an intensity born of desire. And in the quieter passages, Thad's touch softened, a whispered encouragement that drew Billy into an intimate embrace with the music and Liam.

The three men established a deep connection beyond words, communicating only through sound, movement, and touch. They had explored the depths of the piece, with each note taking them deeper and revealing something new, something profound. Finally, as the last chords faded into silence, Billy was left speechless, his body trembling.

Thad reached his arms around Billy, lifted him off the piano bench, turned him around, and embraced him while Liam paced the room to catch his breath. When Thad released Billy, Liam took his place, offering him a sweaty hug; he had tears in his eyes.

When everyone had calmed down, Thad delivered insights, inspirations, and examples to follow and execute. Billy softened as he learned, no longer driven by ego or fear. He gave more. Thad encouraged him to be more playful in the lighter sections of the piece and more deliberate in the dramatic ones.

During a break from rehearsal, Billy chatted and sipped Cokes with Liam.

"The love you've poured into this piece is a testament to

your love for Finn. I love dogs, so I get it. She was a good companion to you. And I appreciate you and Finn, even though I never met her. She's your muse, your guide. You've celebrated her life beautifully and lovingly."

Billy sat looking at Liam, tears meeting in the corners of his eyes when the door to the studio opened. Martha Morgan seemed to float in defiance of gravity just above the ground in an old yet stylish black Halston dress. She looked mystical as she levitated before Billy, an aura of otherworldliness surrounding her. He stood up immediately and faced the renowned choreographer.

"Billy, dear, why don't you take a class with us? It will help you see what it's like to be a dancer and help you better connect with Liam during rehearsals as he choreographs the piece and later while he's performing on stage."

Billy put down his can of Coke and stared at Marsha. He was dumbfounded. Having his music included in the upcoming run was an unbelievable opportunity, but he thought they'd use a professional pianist for the actual performance. Was he up for that kind of pressure? Was he good enough for New York?

"Ms. Morgan, are you saying you want me to perform live? I'm honored, but are you sure?"

"I've been listening during today's rehearsal, and I am confident you can do this. I knew it was special when Thad had you send me a recording of "Transcendence." I do not doubt that you can make this work and bring your unique musical magic to our company. Showcase your talent to our audience."

Right after rehearsal, there was a level-one modern dance class. Billy stayed around for it. Liam reached for a new black leotard in the men's changing room, still in an unopened bag.

"Here, you're going to need these. What you wear in a dance class is important here. Black tights and a white t-shirt are standard."

Billy took the tights as Liam reached for something else from the locker's top shelf. It looked like another garment in an unopened plastic bag: a dance belt.

"Here, you'll need this, too, to keep everything in place." Liam looked down at Billy's crotch to make sure he knew what the dance belt was for. "Look, don't take this the wrong way, but let me know if you need help putting it on or arranging stuff."

Billy's blush shot up his neck and flooded his cheeks. Without eye contact, he mumbled, "No, it's okay. I think I can figure it out." He then tried to offer Liam cash for the gear, but Liam wouldn't hear it.

Billy would see if taking the class would help his playing, and he was eager to experience Morgan's approach to modern technique. Easier said than done, but the floor work alone was the most brutal physical workout he'd ever endured.

Billy liked allowing gravity to keep him grounded during the beginning of the class. He was fine for most of it since he spent so much time writhing on the floor, contracting and releasing in time to the harsh percussive sounds of the piano accompaniment. He was exhausted when he transitioned to the next class segment. But there was no escaping what came next: the across-the-floor sequences. And where he liked gravity, he feared heights. Traveling across the floor doing long running strides, leaps, jetés, and pirouettes felt threatening as each participant was more visible to the other. Billy was embarrassed by how his body moved through space. Something as natural as keeping his arms and legs in opposition as he moved across the room became a struggle. Every movement had to be worked out in his head before executing it; the delay in messaging the routine from the brain to the body made him look like he was dancing to the beat of a completely different drummer. The awkward proof of his lubberly movement was reflected in every mirrored surface in the studio. But his struggle helped him better appreciate what dancers go through to perfect their craft. The empathetic understanding he gained allowed him to become a better partner when rehearsing with Liam. Now, he could appreciate, at least physically, what it meant to suffer for one's art, as clichéd as that sounded.

Chapter 25

Billy and Liam bonded through their respective art forms. During their marathon practice sessions, the concept of time dissolved, and the hours slipped away unnoticed, as if caught in a timeless vortex. Billy and Liam were engulfed by an all-encompassing flow of sound and movement, a rhythm as ancient and unending as human history. In those moments, the world outside ceased to exist, and they were suspended in a realm where only the art of their craft mattered.

While Thad sat in during most rehearsals, taking notes and providing feedback, he would often disappear before the session was over. Billy hoped he and Thad could spend time together, grab a coffee, or have dinner before he returned to Jersey. But mostly, he wanted to dismantle the emotional wall that Thad had erected between them. He tried to tell Thad how he felt about him, how he had felt since their first kiss under the boardwalk, but Thad would always change the subject, talk about work, or find something else to occupy his time.

During one rehearsal, as Thad gave notes to Liam, Billy took a deep breath and approached him. "Thad, when you two take a break, I need to talk to you about something," Billy said, his voice steady but his heart racing.

Thad glanced up, his expression unreadable. "Sure, Billy. What's up?"

"It's about us and what happened that night under the boardwalk," Billy began, his voice wavering slightly.

Thad's eyes darted around the room before settling back on Billy. "Billy, I think we should focus on the work right now. We can talk about personal stuff later," he said, his tone cool and distant.

Billy sighed, feeling the familiar sting of rejection. "Right, work. Got it."

In contrast, Liam was always there to unwind over a meal or on a walk through Central Park after rehearsal. He even offered Billy a place to stay during the month leading up to and throughout the ten days of performances. Billy appreciated this, as it meant less commuting between Manhattan for rehearsals and Beachside for school. They had formed a genuine friendship, and both men cherished it.

Liam could sense the sexual tension between Billy and Thad, and once Billy realized he could trust him, Liam became his confidant in all matters of Billy's unrequited love. Liam shared with him that he thought Thad had romantic feelings for Billy.

One evening, as they sat in Liam's cozy loft after a long day of rehearsals, Liam gently broached the subject.

"Have you talked to Thad about how you feel?" Liam asked, pouring Billy another glass of wine.

Billy sighed, staring into the glass. "I've tried, but he always changes the subject. It's like he's avoiding it on purpose."

Liam nodded thoughtfully. "Maybe he's scared. Sometimes, the person you least expect can be the most afraid of facing their feelings."

Billy looked up, a flicker of hope in his eyes. "You think he feels the same way?"

Liam smiled supportively. "I've seen the way he looks at you, Billy. There's something there. You need to give him time and space to accept it."

On the Friday two weeks before the premiere of Liam and Billy's piece, Billy spent the night at Liam's. Taking advantage of the unusually mild late-fall weather, they bypassed the more convenient 6 train stop near the studio, which would have taken them directly to Union Square. Instead, they strolled through Central Park, exited onto Central Park South, and caught the Q train at Fifty-Seventh Street. Reemerging at Union Square, they walked the rest of the way to Liam's loft in the East Village, passing through neighborhoods coming to life as residents returned home at the end of the workweek.

The air was filled with the vibrant energy of an East Village Friday evening. Local bars and pubs were lively, patrons spilling onto the sidewalks, savoring drinks and laughter in the neon twilight. The inviting atmosphere starkly contrasted with the typical rush of weekday evenings. Small groups gathered outside cafés and bakeries, where the scent of fresh bread and pastries mingled with the crisp fall air. Sidewalks buzzed with people picking up groceries for dinner, tote bags filled with artisanal cheeses and wine, their faces alight with the relief of a week concluded.

Liam lived in a fifth-floor walk-up loft. As a dancer, he appreciated the physical benefits and lower rent of a building without an elevator. The two men maneuvered the narrow stairwell, giggling each time they touched as they climbed the steep, worn steps. The stairs creaked a song of the city's history, blending with the distant sounds of car horns, sidewalk conversations, and the occasional street musician playing a mellow tune on a saxophone.

At the top, exposed brick walls and stunning views of Uptown greeted them. The apartment's open layout was perfect for a dancer, spacious enough to move around without knocking into furniture. Through the large windows the soft, amber glow from sodium vapor street lamps mingled with the cooler, white light cast by new LED replacements. Shop windows' incandescent bulbs, yet to be replaced by more energy-efficient options, reflected off the pavement, adding a magical quality to the scene outside.

"Let me pull something together for supper. Then, if you're up to it, we could go out dancing at Tryst."

Since they had started working together, Billy enjoyed going out with Liam. Although he preferred quieter settings, he wasn't one to shy away from the dance floor, even in the presence of a world-class dancer like Liam. The prospect of mingling with the lively crowd of the East Village, where the night was beginning to unfold, filled him with excitement and anticipation.

"Sure thing. It'd be good to get out and let off some steam."

Liam prepared a quick meal, and after eating, Billy cleaned up. Liam then changed into something more suitable for the night.

Just a block from Liam's loft was Tryst, a gay dance club that catered to a lively and inclusive crowd. It was a place where patrons could freely express themselves through pulsating music and vibrant lighting.

As Liam and Billy crossed Tryst's threshold, the thumping bass reverberated through their bodies, inviting them to join the rhythm on the dance floor below. Before diving into the crowd, Liam spotted a familiar face at the bar and pulled

Billy over to introduce them. The man sported a quintessential Wall Street haircut, the epitome of sharp, polished professionalism. His hair was short and meticulously groomed, with closely cropped sides tapering neatly into the longer, slicked-back top. The precise lines around his ears and neckline highlighted his clean-cut appearance.

As they approached, Marcus turned, his eyes landing on Billy. Recognition lit up his expression, cutting off Liam's attempt to introduce them. "Billy?" Marcus said, a grin spreading across his face.

Billy blinked in surprise; then, a slow smile crept across his face. "Marcus? I didn't expect to run into you here!"

Turning to Liam, Marcus quipped, "This is the talented Billy you've been raving about?" He then turned back to Billy. "He says you're the next big thing in music."

Billy laughed. "That's kind of him to say. Do you come here often?"

Marcus's eyes twinkled with mischief. "Oh, I'm a regular. I can't resist the music and the people. Plus, it's always fun running into old friends and making new ones."

Liam, caught off guard, chuckled. "Wait, you two already know each other?"

Marcus laughed, clapping Billy on the shoulder. "We go way back. We grew up near each other and went to middle and high school together. Small world, huh?"

Liam shook his head in amazement, then quickly bought a round of tequila shots, which they happily downed together as the conversation flowed more easily. The initial surprise gave way to camaraderie.

Billy felt a surge of curiosity and hesitated briefly before asking, "Do you still keep in touch with Pierce?" He recalled the few times when Pierce wasn't hanging out with Jake and Karl; he was usually with Marcus and a saner crowd.

"Not as much as we used to. However, he gave me a late-night call over the summer. He was distraught—believe it or not, he talked about you." Marcus leaned in close, his lips brushing Billy's ear as he continued, "Pierce has always had a thing for you. He just never knew how to express it."

Billy's eyes widened in surprise. "Really? I always thought he was teasing me or trying to make my life difficult."

Marcus shook his head. "Nah, he's just not great at showing his true feelings. He's a bit of a mess, always following the wrong gods home, but he means well—sometimes."

"Yeah, I know what you mean."

"I heard from my parents that he got a job somewhere in the city. He's probably causing his usual ruckus there, too." Marcus exhaled a stilted chuckle.

Billy's mind raced as he connected the dots. Pierce had left a significant mark on him, both physically and emotionally. The thought of him being in the city was unsettling.

The DJ turned up the volume, and the ever-present thud of an intoxicating beat made it nearly impossible for the conversation to continue. Liam pulled Billy onto the dance floor, calling back to Marcus, "Join us?"

"I thought you'd never ask." Marcus closed the distance in a heartbeat, tearing off his shirt in one fluid motion and tucking it into the waistband of his jeans.

Billy's eyes roamed over Marcus, taking in the sight of his broad, sculpted chest. This wasn't the skinny, geeky boy he remembered from the high school locker room. Marcus's physical metamorphosis was impressive. A striking bear tattoo spread across his left pectoral, while a bull occupied his right, facing each other and fighting for dominance. His well-defined pectoral muscles stood out prominently, complementing a perfect six-pack with deep valleys of muscle as if his body were finely chiseled from marble. Below his right ribcage, an intricate compass tattoo symbolized his inner drive and constant quest for direction.

Even amidst the pulsating energy of the dance floor, his hair retained a sleek finish, reflecting a disciplined routine. Broad shoulders tapered into sinewy arms, veins tracing intricate patterns beneath his smooth, tanned skin. A sleeve of tattoos adorned his left arm, featuring international financial symbols and geometric designs that hinted at his analytical mind. The V-shaped taper from his shoulders to his narrow waist created an erotic silhouette, and a small city skyline tattoo on his lower back subtly referenced his urban life. His back muscles undulated with fluid precision as he joined the other men, tattoos shifting like an animated tapestry with hypnotic grace.

In the protection of the circle of men around them, they moved in perfect harmony, their bodies synced with the energetic, upbeat tempo of the music. Their movements were effortless, the same kind of effortlessness that Billy and Liam had come to expect from each other during rehearsals at the studio. With Marcus adding his unique style to the mix, the trio radiated a magnetic energy that drew admiring glances from the crowd.

The music seamlessly transitioned between house, techno, trance, and dubstep, offering an infectious variety that catered to all. As the music reached its crescendo, Liam spun Billy around, their chests pressed tightly together, their breaths mingling in the humid, sweat-tinged air. Liam reached out and pulled Marcus into their embrace. Their eyes locked in joyful celebration, and to onlookers, the three men might have seemed like passionate lovers caught in a heated, lustful gaze. But that wasn't the case; Billy and Liam had become close friends through their collaborative work. Their platonic love was grounded in companionship, trust, and mutual respect. Convincing the crowd that they were simply three friends enjoying the moment and not an alluring polyamorous threesome would be a challenge.

Their celebration on the dance floor intensified, bodies sweating and gleaming under the disco's strobing lights. The crowd around them cheered and whistled, caught up in the electrifying energy of their dancing.

An hour later, with one last round of shots, Billy and Liam said goodbye to Marcus, who had called it a night. The two men climbed to one of the balconies to catch their breath. They sat down, still shirtless, with the overactive air conditioning cooling their sweat-drenched bodies.

"That was amazing," Billy said, his voice barely audible over the pulsating music.

Liam nodded, grinning. "You were amazing, Billy. You've got some moves."

Billy laughed, the tension of the past few weeks melting away. "Thanks, but I'll stick to playing the piano. It was good to reunite with Marcus, too, and so cool that you know him."

Liam's expression softened as he looked at Billy and changed the subject. "You know, you should talk to Thad again. Don't let him slip away without knowing how you truly feel."

Billy sighed, staring out over the dance floor. "I just don't know if he feels the same way," he said.

Liam placed a reassuring hand on Billy's shoulder. "You won't know until you ask. You've got to take that risk, Billy. For his sake and for yours."

Billy nodded, feeling a renewed determination. "You're right. I'll talk to him."

They watched the crowd below, savoring a moment of peace amidst the vibrant energy around them. Once they had collected themselves, they headed back to Liam's loft. As they walked through the quiet streets of the East Village, Billy felt hopeful. Maybe things would work out with Thad after all. He had to believe that a relationship with Thad was worth fighting for, and despite the late hour, Billy felt re-energized.

Once inside, Liam and Billy kicked off their shoes, the night's adventures still humming in their bones. The energy of Tryst had given way to a soothing stillness, the kind that only follows hours of celebrating and laughter. They moved around the loft with a practiced ease, an unspoken rhythm born from countless nights spent together as friends and col-laborators.

Liam glanced at the queen-sized bed, a simple yet inviting piece of furniture nestled in the corner of his spacious loft. "You know the drill," he said, tossing Billy a spare pair of sweatpants. "We'll just have to share again."

Billy caught the sweatpants with a grateful smile and slipped into the comfortable fabric. "Thanks, Liam. By the way, how do you know Marcus? You two seemed pretty tight."

Liam paused, a thoughtful smile playing on his lips as he peeled off his shirt and pants, changing into his sleepwear. "Yeah, we actually dated for a short while. It was intense but brief. We realized we were better off as friends and have kept in touch since then. It's nice to have someone who understands the club scene and the importance of a healthy relationship."

Billy nodded, a smile forming on his lips. "That's cool. It's good to have friends who get you, especially in this place." Liam's smile widened, showing appreciation for his friendship with Billy.

The bed beckoned them with crisp white sheets and a cozy down comforter. They climbed in, Liam on one side and Billy on the other, the mattress sinking slightly under their combined weight. Liam pulled the comforter up, enveloping them both in a cocoon of warmth. He turned to Billy, their faces close enough to feel the other's breath in the cool air.

"Hey, you know you're safe here, right?" Liam's voice was soft, his eyes sincere. "Sharing a bed doesn't mean more than just getting some sleep."

Billy nodded, a soft chuckle escaping his lips. "Yeah, I know. It's nice. It's been a long time since I felt this comfortable with someone."

Liam's smile spread across his face. "Same here. It's nice not to have to pretend, you know? Just two friends sharing a space, nothing more."

They lay there in silence for a moment, the dim glow of the city lights filtering through the loft's windows and casting a soft luminescence over them. The sounds of the city provided a comforting backdrop, a lullaby of distant traffic and murmured conversations that merged with the rhythmic beating of their hearts.

Liam reached over and gently squeezed Billy's hand. "Good night, Billy. You're doing great; you know that?"

Billy squeezed back, a smile forming on his lips. "Thanks, Liam. Good night."

They turned onto their sides, facing away from each

other. The space between them was filled with the comforting knowledge that true friendship transcended the need for anything more physical. Wrapped in the weight of the comforter and the closeness of their friendship, they drifted off to sleep, knowing that the bond they shared was unshakeable, rooted in respect and mutual understanding.

The following day, Billy woke up early and made breakfast for both of them. As they ate, Liam encouraged him again. "Remember, Billy, you deserve to be happy. Don't settle for anything less."

Billy nodded, thankful for his friend's support and strength.

Chapter 26

Thad went to the back of the house for "Transcendence." He paced behind the standing-room-only crowd under the mezzanine overhang. At the concert grand piano, stage right, a soft halo of ambient light swathed Billy in an ethereal aura that seemed to emanate from him rather than from the rigging above. He wore a sleek, black satin shirt fitted to his form and subtly unbuttoned at the top, the fabric catching the light with a soft sheen. Tailored black velvet trousers added texture, contrasting the satin's luster, while polished leather shoes and a simple pearl choker around his neck completed his look with understated allure. At first, it looked as if he was alone on the stage. But he wasn't alone; Liam, dressed in a form-fitting black mesh top that revealed glimpses of his toned physique, paired with black neoprene trunks subtly patterned to catch the light, knelt in the center stage darkness. Motionless, arms and hands draped around his head, he embodied an unseen downward force as he anticipated Billy's opening notes. The combination of mesh, neoprene, and bare skin made his stillness even more captivating under the complex lighting.

Seeing the two men together, two men he adored for different reasons, brought Thad a feeling of pride—and also something else, maybe envy. He marveled at how well they all had connected from the very first time they worked together, their ability to merge their art forms into an act of mesmerizing beauty and perfection. No, it was more than envy. What he felt was jealousy. He blushed, ashamed to admit it to himself. But no one could see his embarrassment tucked away in the darkness. He hoped the red glow from the exit sign over the door neutralized his condition. The only person who noticed was an usher resting against a doorjamb when she shined her tiny flashlight in his face to see if he needed help finding his seat.

There was a time when Liam had pursued him relentlessly, always bringing him his favorite coffee during rehearsals, frothed just how he liked it. He was even bold enough to ask Thad out on dates numerous times. He was crazy in love with Thad, or so he said. And Thad was interested, but in Thad's repetitive chaste mantras of *I-don't-have-time-for-this* and *I-have-my-career-to-think-about*, he'd lost Liam to others more intent on building a meaningful relationship, a future together.

The music began as stratified layers of shadow and light shot across the stage from the wings, their horizontal effect accentuating the dancer's movements and enhancing the weight pressing down on Liam. The music serpentined through the complex lighting pattern, guiding Liam through a symbolic encounter with the frozen river. He harnessed the full force of gravity to the delight of the mesmerized audience, moving into the blackness of the stage floor as if his body became intangible, slipping through the surface to a darker realm, only to reappear transformed.

Thad felt like he was witnessing a superhero in the flesh, the way Superman, Shadowcat, or Martian Manhunter could phase through solid walls and objects. Or, he was watching a ghost moving about, unconcerned about physical limitations;

either way, the effect was breathtaking.

As the music surged into the coda, the atmosphere on stage underwent a dramatic shift. Once carefully delineated, the stratified layers of shadow and light dissolved into a cascade of shimmering particles, morphing into a torrent of opaque glitter that rained down from above, only to vanish upon contact with the floor—a marvel of technical theater magic.

Now fully illuminated, Liam stood center stage, his form seemingly more powerful and ethereal, as if the darker realm he passed through had imbued him with new strength. The intensity of his movements increased, each gesture sharp and purposeful, embodying the raw energy that had been building throughout the performance.

Billy, too, was in full light. Their synchrony complete; their movements and sound seamlessly joined—a perfect harmony. The audience experienced the connection between the two, a dynamic interplay of forces—Liam's transformed self now moved with reborn fluidity. At the same time, Billy partnered him on the piano with complementary grace.

The stage went black. Silence enveloped the entire theater. It felt, at least for the time it would take Billy and Liam to exhale in the release of their performance and for the lights to come back up, that no one was in the theater but Thad. That's how quiet it was.

He could only begin to imagine what the two men sitting in darkness waiting for the audience's audible reaction were feeling. Then the applause came, more thunderous than any other piece performed that night. The lights came up on the stage for their bow as the two men faced a standing ovation; even from Thad's location at the back of the house, he could see both smiles and tears on the faces of the people nearby.

Thad had worried that the work's inherent sadness could become saccharine melancholy if it weren't executed properly. But it never took that turn; instead, even in rehearsals, it was more of a loving longing for something that no longer existed, a feeling akin to the Welsh word, hiraeth, a form of homesickness over the loss of someone, something, or a place that no longer existed. Through Billy's masterful composition and virtuosity on the piano, and Liam's supreme aesthetic athleticism, they expressed the loyal bond between Billy and Finn. Now, Finn lived on in the hearts of thousands of theatergoers who had witnessed this masterpiece throughout its Broadway run.

Thad returned backstage before the final ensemble piece. Something had changed after what he'd just experienced. Something beyond rational thought, his feeling of hiraeth, something he didn't even realize he'd been missing or waiting for, perhaps his entire life. He needed to talk with Billy, and he needed to do it before it was too late.

Chapter 27

Billy, Marsha Morgan, Thad, Liam Mercer, and the rest of the dance company navigated carefully down the three steps to the garden-level entrance of Curtain Call on West Forty-Sixth Street. Billy's dad had made the trip into the city, even booking a hotel room for the special occasion. He escorted Viktoria and Misty Drizzle, one on each arm, as the trio made a memorable entrance. However, Misty's hoop skirt barely fit through the door, and navigating the narrow space between tables turned into a comedic ballet as they tried to avoid hitting patrons and furniture with the hoop's swing and sway.

The restaurant, carved out of an old brownstone, resembled other restaurants on the block from the outside. Still, Curtain Call was a hidden gem known for its eclectic menu, intimate atmosphere, and frequent celebrity sightings. It was in the heart of New York City's bustling Theater District on Restaurant Row, just a stone's throw away from the iconic Broadway stages.

The interior was adorned with current and vintage Broadway posters, hits and flops, autographed headshots, tabletop candles, and cozy booths, creating the perfect setting for a pre-theater meal or after-show celebration. From mouth-watering steaks and fresh seafood to innovative vegetarian options, there was something to satisfy every craving.

Alongside the restaurant was a narrow alley flanked by aged brick walls and lined with trash bins and graffiti. At first sight, it might be seen as a place to avoid for fear of being mugged, but in reality, the space had become an unofficial backstage area for the kitchen crew and performers alike. Here, wait staff and line cooks took quick cigarette breaks while chorus boys and girls caught up with each other between shows to run lines, share news of upcoming auditions, or enjoy a moment of respite from the footlights. Curtain Call was not just a restaurant; it was an experience—a place where the magic of Broadway extended beyond the stage and into the street.

This was Billy's favorite spot in the city. It was his hangout, even before his involvement with Marsha and her company. He'd drop in for a beer and the restaurant's famous Backstage Burger anytime he popped into the city to catch a matinee or evening performance, sometimes with Viktoria and other times with his fellow teachers when they'd rent a bus to see a show together. Usually, after a matinee, especially when he was alone, he'd sit at the bar for hours, chatting up the bartender for theater gossip or listening to strays nursing their drinks and rambling on about their lives in Connecticut and stock portfolios, the ones who remained behind to supposedly pay the tab after their families headed off for an evening performance—the strays who habitually arrived at shows after the curtain, causing deep sighs and glares from interrupted actors, audience members, dissatisfied wives, and embarrassed kids.

Billy shared his discovery of Curtain Call with Thad, who quickly fell in love with the place. Thad was familiar with Restaurant Row and the Broadway scene. Still, the dance company typically performed at Lincoln Center, so he'd usually eat in that neighborhood or near his apartment in the West Village. However, this season, the company secured a limited engagement at one of the available Broadway houses, and Curtain Call was the perfect spot for the after-party. Besides this gathering being a celebration for the dance company, it was also Billy's night to have his composition premiered, and he was thrilled that his achievement was well-received by the audience, dancers, and Marsha Morgan herself. But Billy was even more taken by Thad's behind-the-scenes planning to hold the party here. It was time to kick back, enjoy food and drinks, and celebrate with his friends and colleagues.

Billy's eyes sparkled with laughter as he happily signed Playbills alongside a few others from the company. Making his way to the long table reserved for them in the center of the room, he felt a strong camaraderie. As soon as they were all seated, he excused himself, "Back in a sec."

Billy navigated through the bustling restaurant, his thoughts lingering on the evening's performance. His steps faltered as he approached the restroom hallway and spotted a familiar face he wasn't particularly pleased to see. "Pierce? What are you doing here?"

Pierce looked just as shocked, his face contorted with surprise and unease. "Oh my god, Billy! This is my restaurant. I work here."

"Since when?" Billy's tone was sharp, unable to mask his surprise.

"Since today," Pierce replied, trying to keep his voice steady. "To be honest, I've been here for a week. This is the job I told you I had lined up for the fall back in the summer."

Billy nodded, forced politeness masking his true feelings. Then he added, "Piss off any staff yet?"

Pierce shrugged, letting Billy know he had, and then deflected the accusation. "I've heard about your recent success working with that dance company. Congratulations, Billy."

"Yeah, Thad's been amazing," Billy responded, though his mind was elsewhere. "He needed a piece of music to round out the dance company's program, and I had just the music he wanted."

The mention of Thad deflated Pierce. "Billy, can we talk for a moment? Somewhere more private?"

Billy hesitated but then nodded. He didn't care for Pierce's tone but followed him into the alley, away from unwanted attention. Pierce cleared his throat, the air thick with tension.

"Billy, I was completely out of line in the summer. I'm asking for your forgiveness. Again. I want to start over now that I'm settled in the city and have this great chef's job. What do you say? Or are you in love with the musical genius? Before you came over here, I watched him chatting up that one hot dancer. Does he even know you left the table?"

Billy felt a surge of anger but kept his composure. "That's none of your business with whom I'm in love. And there's no way I'm interested in pursuing a friendship with you or anything else you might have in mind. No way. But to be clear, Thad and I are not more than friends." Billy wanted to say more but he kept it short. "Again, that's none of your business."

Pierce pressed further. "Well then, that's good because I'm telling you there's something between Thad and that dancer guy. I see how close they are, how intimate their conversation looks."

"He's talking to Liam, the company's principal dancer. He works closely with Thad. It is nothing unusual to be that close in a crowded restaurant. Please don't read too much into it. Not everybody's a shameless flirt like you. Thad's not interested in Liam that way."

Pierce reached out and gently touched Billy's arm. "I just want you to be happy, Billy."

"Don't you mean that *you* just want to be happy? I feel sorry for you, Pierce."

"Don't you worry about me; I'm doing just fine. But if you ever need someone to talk to, I'm here."

"That's not gonna happen, Pierce."

Billy turned away, a heavy sigh escaping as he sadly realized he'd have to find a new favorite hangout now that Pierce worked here. He could see in Pierce's eyes that he harbored a glimmer of hope that their paths might cross again, as if, given a chance, he could prove to Billy that he could be a better friend or perhaps something more. But Billy knew it would demand a monumental effort on Pierce's part. He wondered if the man could even muster the time and energy required to turn over a new leaf. Pierce's charm only went so far before it soured. Despite his earnest intentions to become a better man, he always seemed to slip back into his familiar patterns of anger and meanness. Billy began seeing Pierce as nothing more than lonely and bitter. Billy trudged back toward the restaurant, leaving Pierce standing alone in the alley beneath the unforgiving glare of the old mercury-vapor streetlamp when the door to the alley opened.

"There you are." Liam peeked out of the door. "We've been looking for you, Billy, and I also needed to pee, which I did. And now I've found you. Two successes in one trip."

"Liam, I was just coming in." Billy looked unnerved as he pushed past Pierce, while Pierce appeared far more bothered and distraught.

"Is everything all right?" Liam eyed both men's faces. "What did I interrupt?"

In their newfound friendship, Billy had confided in Liam about Pierce—the same Pierce that Marcus knew—and the turmoil he had caused during the summer. Billy could see in Liam's expression that he was concerned. In their short time working together on "Transcendence," which was just a month, Liam had become protective of Billy and tended to look out for him, whether in the dance studio or out on the street.

"Liam, this is an old acquaintance of mine, a former high school classmate, Pierce Talon; he's the chef here, the one that Marcus was talking about at Tryst." He didn't have to remind Liam who the man was or his ties to Billy; it registered on his face. "Pierce, this is Liam Mercer, Marsha Morgan's principal dancer and my friend."

"Pierce." Liam reached over to shake Pierce's reluctant hand. No one could miss the strain between Billy and Pierce's expressions, lingering remnants of what could have only been an intense discussion. He turned back to Billy. "Let's get you back to the party. You can't celebrate your success out here."

Billy joined Liam, arms around each other's shoulders like old friends, and returned to the restaurant. Pierce remained as a rat dragged a slice of bruised pizza across the alley; its pepperoni had long since scraped away like prematurely picked-off scabs on barely healed wounds.

When Billy and Liam rejoined the party in the dining room, Billy recognized the actor currently in the role of Miss Hannigan from an *Annie* revival. After curtains fell and lights dimmed in the theater district, cast members often filled their favorite Restaurant Row haunts, becoming one with fans who had just laid out a few hundred dollars to see them from a distance. At Curtain Call, some performers, those who could play, would take turns at the piano; some even sang hits from their shows to the thrill of customers. As Billy passed the piano, the inebriated Hannigan slipped off the bench and slid under the instrument. Billy and Liam ran over, fell to their knees, and dragged the woozy woman out of her predicament. Fortunately, few diners noticed the woman in her drunken stupor, which was good for her as recent rumors were swirling that could jeopardize her career and impact ticket sales, God forbid.

Billy and Liam firmly, yet discreetly, navigated the woman through the maze of tables and back to her seat in a corner banquette. The two men returned to their party, but Liam addressed the group before sitting down, putting Billy on the spot.

"Let's have Billy play us a song now that the piano is free."

The crowd applauded and said, "Yes, Billy, please play for us," and "We love you, Billy."

"Okay, I'll do it, one song, but only if my dear friend, Viktoria, will sing."

Billy scanned the room for Viktoria and spotted her sitting with Billy's dad. Never one to miss an opportunity, she rose to her feet and sashayed to the piano.

Billy sat at the piano, and Viktoria gripped the live mic, cupping her hand over the head so they could pick a song. She whispered to Billy, "Let's do 'The Object of My Affection'. I think it's perfect for tonight." Billy agreed; it was one of their favorite songs to do together, and it included audience participation when the audience raised their napkins and waved them high above their heads three times during the repetitive "Rosy red" refrain.

Viktoria launched into her shtick. "What a wonderful evening. Now, I'll need your help with this song. You'll need a handkerchief or use your table napkins like this." She pulled out the handkerchief she always kept in her cleavage and waved it to the crowd. The partygoers, the rest of the diners, and the servers eagerly did as they were told.

Billy raised his head to take in the diners and friends all singing along; even his father, Big Billy, and Marsha Morgan, cloth napkin wedged in her crooked hand, joined in. His eyes then found Thad's, and they locked into each other. Billy was carried away by the intense look in the other man's gaze. Something was different, and now, he needed to discover that difference.

When the song ended, some dancers and crew collected their coats and belongings and headed home. The rest of the diners settled their tabs and ran out into the cold. Marsha approached Billy and extended a hand in a parting gesture, Billy taking hold, careful not to press too hard on her knotted fingers.

"What a wonderful night, Billy. I've adored spending time with your delightful father, Big Billy—such a dear. But you and me, we're partners now. I'm expecting great things from you in the future."

Billy blushed. He was nearly overwhelmed with how things had changed in a short time. It all seemed unreal; so much he'd have to process once he returned to his apartment in Beachside. He'd miss the train to the Jersey Shore if he didn't get moving. He checked his phone; it was nearly one in the morning, and the last train left in thirty-five minutes. Not that he *had* to go home—he needed to be in the city for the Saturday performance. His dad had booked a hotel room and offered the pull-out sofa bed if needed. He could crash at Liam's or stay with Victoria at her city friend's apartment. But he wanted to get home, if only for a few hours, just for the solitude. But he'd barely make it if he didn't leave immediately. He offered a quick exit speech to the few remaining revelers and opened the half door to the coat room to search for his jacket.

"Wait. Don't go, Billy." Thad joined Billy inside the coat room. "Don't go. It's so late, come back and stay with me. You don't have school tomorrow; it's Saturday. And why return to Jersey when we have an evening performance tomorrow night?"

Billy's pulse shot up. Could this be the invitation he'd been waiting for since their kiss under the boardwalk, and the on-and-off flirting during rehearsals over the last few weeks? Would this be the opportunity he had hoped for and finally be able to say the things he needed to speak to Thad without interruption?

Chapter 28

The air thickened with unresolved emotions once they arrived at Thad's apartment. Billy glanced around, his eyes betraying urgency and apprehension. "Thad, I need to make a quick call...in private," he said, barely above a whisper.

Thad furrowed his brows. "Who do you need to speak to at this late hour?" he asked but immediately shook his head. "Never mind, it's none of my business. You can call from the courtyard."

Billy nodded gratefully, his heart pounding, and went out to the back courtyard. The chill of the night air prickled his skin, starkly contrasting the heat of his racing thoughts. With trembling fingers, he dialed Curtain Call's number, hoping against hope that someone would pick up.

As the phone rang, Billy glanced up at the starry sky above, a silent prayer on his lips. It was late, past two in the morning, but maybe someone was still there, tidying up the restaurant for Saturday. After all, he was in a city that never slept, just like him, unable to rest with so much happening between tonight's premiere, his encounter with Pierce in the alley, and hoping he'd finally have an intimate night with Thad.

Billy glanced through the window into the apartment. Thad paced restlessly, fluffing and chopping throw pillows each time he passed by the couch. Billy wondered if Thad felt the same way about him as he did for Thad. He wanted a relationship with Thad beyond mere friendship. Billy hoped that Thad could rid himself of the stubbornness that fueled his false claim of not dating as a way to maintain independence for the sake of his career.

Suddenly, a voice broke through the silence, bringing Billy out of his reverie. Billy's call connected, and the dishwasher answered.

"Curtain Call. We're closed. Call back tomorrow."

"Wait, wait, wait!" Billy shouted into his cell phone. "Don't hang up, please. Is Pierce still around? I need to speak to him."

"Hold on, buddy, I think I can get him."

Billy heard the man call out, "Telephone for you."

The conversation with Pierce was short and to the point, almost over before it began. Billy said precisely what Pierce wanted to hear. He hung up.

If love were worth fighting for with Thad, even if it risked rejection and heartache, he'd have to take care of this one obstacle before he could move forward. Tonight, right now, he would remove that obstacle, and he hoped that Thad would understand.

When Billy returned from the courtyard, Thad looked anxious. Since their coat room conversation just an hour ago, Billy knew Thad wanted to talk to him about something. Billy knew this was the moment they had both been waiting for, and he hoped that what they wanted to say to each other could wait until he got back.

Chapter 29

Pierce headed out to the alley, about to walk back to his Hell's Kitchen apartment when the dishwasher called after him. He held the kitchen's landline receiver in the air, soapy water spiraling down his forearms, dripping from his elbow, and running along the coiled cord.

"Telephone, for you."

The dishwasher snatched the towel tucked into his apron, wiped down the phone, and handed it to Pierce. He had no idea who might be calling him so late.

The call was brief. Pierce hung up the phone. The dishwasher, who had just finished rinsing the last pot and hung it on the suspended utility rack above the cooktop, turned to Pierce with concern in his eyes.

"Everything all right, chef?"

"Everything's fine, perfect, in fact." Pierce's smile wiped away any concern from the other man's face.

Pierce said good night for the second time that evening and headed toward his apartment. Once out of the alley and onto Forty-Sixth Street, he quickened his pace until he found himself running. He ran all the way home. Once there, he stripped off his chef's whites and black-and-white houndstooth work pants and jumped into the shower.

His excitement grew as he soaped away the stew of cooking

smells and grease lingering on his skin after a long night in the kitchen. The warm water traced his skin, an exquisite fusion of rich chestnut and honeyed alabaster that glistened in the steam, each droplet caressing his body before slipping away. He toweled off and carefully chose his attire. He pulled out a pair of red trunks but second-guessed himself, thinking they were too sexy, and opted for skimpy emerald green briefs instead. The stretching fabric clung snugly, accentuating every curve, every contour of his narrow waist, crotch, and well-defined ass. The effect of the color against his skin was vibrant and luxurious. Over them, he draped an open robe, leaving little to the imagination. He wanted to make an impression. He'd waited so long for this opportunity and didn't want to blow it.

The intercom let him know when his night visitor had arrived. He buzzed him in. He'd lost control of the flutter of nerves he was trying so hard to contain. He's here. He'd longed for this moment, to be alone with him and finally express his feelings without inhibition or someone in the way. No Thad or that other guy, the one who had acted like a mosquito in the alley earlier tonight. Liam. What a pest.

Pierce considered how to greet him: leave the door closed so he'd have to knock and then greet Billy up close, his robe open, revealing flesh? Was that too much, too soon? How about lighting a candle, lighting ten candles? Maybe he was trying too hard. He opted for a simple but tasteful staging like realtors do when trying to sell a multimillion-dollar listing to a meticulous client. Still, he'd need to be subtle—again, nothing over the top. It had to look natural.

He opened the door so that Billy could walk right in; then, he ran back into the kitchen to grab a bottle of wine, a Zinfandel, and two glasses. He placed them on the coffee table, dimmed the lights, and arranged himself in the middle of his leather sofa; robe splayed open so that Billy could discover him all casual-like as if this was normal, how he was at home. Perfect, he figured, classy and down-to-earth all at once.

Billy appeared at the door, still wearing his clothes from his performance and celebratory night out. This is it. He took a deep breath, willing himself to remain composed. He remained seated on the couch, thinking, let him come to me.

"Hey, Billy," Pierce said, his voice betraying none of the turmoil within. "Come on in. Hang your coat up by the door."

He watched as Billy's gaze swept over him, taking in his lack of attire. Was he impressed? He couldn't quite tell. He kept his topcoat on.

"I've been looking forward to this," Pierce admitted, his tone laced with more than a hint of seduction. "Just the two of us, finally getting a chance to talk."

"Yes, Pierce, we need to talk." Billy's voice was steady but held an underlying tension. He searched the room as if looking for a place to sit. Pierce patted the cushion next to him, a not-so-subtle invitation to join him on the couch. Billy stood and continued, "I can't keep doing this, Pierce."

"Doing what, Billy? Some wine?" Pierce poured two glasses of Zinfandel and clumsily lifted the glass to his lips. As he tilted the glass back, a dribble escaped the corner of his mouth, trickling down his chin. With an embarrassed chuckle, he hastily wiped his face with the back of his hand, leaving a streak of crimson across his cheek. His lips curled into a sheepish grin. "Aah. So good. Have some, Billy." When Billy didn't respond, Pierce's expression faltered. Any warmth he might have felt from the wine was no match for the unyielding coldness in Billy's eyes. A flicker of hurt flashed across Pierce's features before he quickly masked it with a sly grin. "Oh, Billy, always so serious," he scoffed, though there was a hint of desperation in his tone. "Can't we just enjoy each other's company without all this heavy talk?"

"I'm sorry, Pierce," Billy said softly, meeting his gaze with resolve. "But I can't keep doing this dance with you. It's time for me to break free of you once and forever. This can't be good for you either."

Pierce felt the tension crackling between them. He wanted to reach out, to pull him close and confess everything that'd been weighing on his mind for so long, since that winter morning on the river when Billy cried out to him for help. When he did nothing to help, he'd held back, concerned more about how his friends, Jake and Karl, would react if he dared to go to Billy's aid. He feared he'd scare Billy off and ruin this opportunity to get closer if he brought that incident up along with all the others he needed to apologize for.

Instead, he tried to play it cool, masking his insecurities behind a facade of charm and charisma, his go-to defense. But deep down, he knew the truth. He was terrified of losing Billy, of driving him away with his jealousy and possessiveness.

Billy stood there, staring at him, waiting for him to reply, but Pierce didn't know how to start or what words to scrabble together to say what he wanted. He wasn't used to feeling like this, vulnerable and exposed. He glanced down at his attire, or lack thereof, and suddenly became self-conscious. He pulled the robe closed, the emerald green briefs peeking out as a reminder of what lay beneath. When he did, Billy sat down in the chair across from him.

"Pierce, the fact is, there is no us. I'll admit that I liked and was attracted to you in high school. I thought I saw something in you that indicated maybe you felt the same way. But you became someone else whenever you were with Jake and Karl."

Pierce sank deeper into the sofa. "Billy, can't we just forget about all that?"

"No, Pierce. I can't just forget about it. Your actions hurt me deeply, back then and now."

"Fine. What do you want me to say?"

"I want you to acknowledge how you treated me and made me feel like I wasn't worthy of being myself."

"It wasn't like that, Billy. You don't understand the pressure I was under."

"I understand more than you think. But that doesn't excuse your behavior."

"You're right. I messed up. I should have helped you save your dog. I was a real shit to you that day."

"Yes, you were. And you walking away that morning when I needed you hurt badly, but not as badly as the pain of losing Finn. That dog meant everything to me, Pierce."

"I was scared that if I helped you, people would know how I felt about you. Jake and Karl would know."

"And that fear caused you to hurt me."

Pierce's voice broke. "I know, Billy. I'm sorry. I was a coward. I'm so sorry about Finn."

"I appreciate the apology, but that was years ago. I'll never forget that dog and what she meant to me, and I've worked through that loss. But there's everything else you've done. It adds up, Pierce. You seem so caught up in jealousy and rage whenever I'm around. It doesn't matter if months or years go by between running into each other. It's always the same with you."

"Billy, please. I love you. I've always loved you. I've been in love with you since high school. When I saw you with Thad, it drove me crazy. I couldn't stand the thought of you being with someone else, someone better. I wanted to be the one to make you happy, but I didn't know how."

Billy took a deep breath, his eyes softening with sorrow and determination. "But understand, Pierce, this isn't just about us. It's about you finding your way."

Pierce looked down, his voice barely above a whisper. "I don't know how to do that."

Billy stared at Pierce. "Love isn't always enough, Pierce, especially when mixed with jealousy and possessiveness. It's not healthy for either of us."

Pierce nodded, fussing with the sash on his robe, and continued staring at the floor.

"I mean it. Look at me, Pierce."

Pierce raised his head and looked directly at him.

"I'm happy for you for getting that job at Curtain Call. I know you've worked hard for it. You're good at what you do in the kitchen. But it's my favorite place in the city, and I'm not letting you ruin it for me. So, unless you can behave when I'm there, it'll be as if I don't know you, that you don't exist for me at all. Do you understand?"

Pierce considered Billy's words carefully. A small smile crossed his lips, exposing his perfect teeth. He sat up a bit and spoke.

"I can do that; at least I can try."

"Thanks, Pierce, that's all I'm asking."

"Can I ask you something?"

"Sure, what do you want to ask me?"

"Do you think we can ever be friends?"

"That's up to you. You'll have to earn it, Pierce. And you'll have to figure out how on your own."

Pierce's full smile returned. He took a sip of wine and gestured toward Billy's untouched glass.

"No thanks. It's late. I've got to go." Billy stood to leave.

Pierce also stood and walked around the coffee table to face Billy, carefully keeping his robe closed.

Billy continued, "Oh, and one more thing. If I saw you dressed like this back in high school and somehow we were alone together, I don't know if I could have contained myself. Who knows what would've happened? You were beautiful then, and you're beautiful now."

"Wait, are you flirting with me?"

"No, not flirting, just stating a fact."

"Thanks, Billy; I appreciate that. I hope that someone else can see through my nonsense someday. I am so tired of being alone."

"It'll happen, Pierce. Try a little empathy and be willing to take the time to build a healthy relationship when you find that special someone. And he's out there for you, trust me."

"How are you doing with that?"

"Still working on that, Pierce, but I'm hopeful."

"How about a hug?" Pierce reached out to hug him, but Billy raised his hand, derailing the embrace.

"Not ready for that, but I'm glad we could talk things through tonight. Good night, Pierce."

"Good night, Billy." Pierce hesitated and began to ask, "Uh, Billy...?"

"Good night, Pierce," Billy repeated and left the apartment.

As Billy left, Pierce felt clarity. Their conversation stirred something deep within him, inspiring him to change.

Determined to act on this newfound motivation, Pierce grabbed a pen and some paper. He began sketching plans for a small dinner event for the restaurant's staff at Curtain Call, thinking of ways to showcase a softer, more collaborative side of himself and show them what he could do in the kitchen.

He jotted down ideas for the menu and considered how he could create an atmosphere that encouraged teamwork and camaraderie. Along with the dinner plans, he made a list of colleagues he needed to apologize to, starting with one he had previously clashed with.

Pierce decided to share his plans with the staff the next day. He would apologize to the colleague he had wronged and explain his intention to join a support group to work on his anger and jealousy issues. He hoped his colleagues would be surprised by the meal he had personally prepared for them and appreciative of his newfound attitude.

This transformation wouldn't happen overnight, and he knew that, but Pierce was determined to make a genuine effort. This new purpose and desire for redemption gave him hope for the future, opening the door to a new dynamic with Billy and others.

Chapter 30

Billy returned to Thad's apartment feeling relieved. The conversation with Pierce had been draining but necessary. Now, he had to face Thad and the unresolved feelings that had been simmering between them for months.

Thad looked up from the couch as Billy entered, his eyes reflecting many emotions—concern, curiosity, and perhaps something Billy hoped was longing.

"Everything okay?" Thad asked, his voice filled with genuine concern.

"Yeah," Billy sighed, running a hand through his hair. "It's done. I just needed to clear some things up with Pierce."

Thad nodded, and Billy could see the tension in his shoulders ease slightly. "I'm glad. I'm sorry he's been a problem for you."

Billy gave a small, tired smile. "It's been a long night."

Thad stood up and moved closer, his gaze softening as he looked at Billy. "You want to talk about it?"

Billy shook his head. "No, not really. I want to forget about it, at least for tonight."

Thad hesitated for a moment before gently touching Billy's arm. "Then let's focus on us. I've wanted to talk to you, too."

Billy's heart skipped a beat. "About what?"

"About us," Thad said, his voice barely above a whisper. "About what's been happening between us."

Billy swallowed hard, his pulse quickening. "Thad, I—"

"Wait," Thad interrupted, taking a deep breath. "Let me go first."

Billy nodded, ready for whatever he was about to hear.

Thad moved closer, his fingers brushing Billy's arm with a tentative, electric touch. "I've tried to ignore it, to pretend I feel nothing more than friendship. But I can't keep lying to myself, Billy. I want more."

Billy's breath hitched, a thrill of hope unfurling in his chest. He searched Thad's eyes, finding only sincerity and longing.

"I've waited so long to hear that," Billy confessed, his voice unsteady. "But I was scared you didn't feel the same."

Thad's grip on Billy's arm tightened slightly, grounding them both. "I do, Billy. I've always felt it. I didn't know how to risk what we have."

Billy took a step closer, closing the distance between them. "Sometimes you have to risk it to get what you want."

Thad's eyes darkened with resolve. "Are you ready to take that risk with me?"

Billy's response was wordless, a nod suffused with certainty. A smile spread across his face. "Yes, Thad. I'm ready."

Thad cupped Billy's face, drawing him into a kiss that spoke of all the words left unsaid. The moment stretched, every touch and breath affirming the feelings they'd both kept hidden. When they finally pulled back, Thad rested his forehead against Billy's, a playful light in his eyes.

"I've wanted to do that for so long," he murmured.

"Me too," Billy whispered, his breath mingling with

Thad's. "And to think, I'm keeping this old man on his toes."

Thad chuckled, the tension between them easing with the shared humor. "Old man? Really? Six years isn't that much, you know."

Billy grinned. "Maybe not, but you always did have that distinguished look."

"Distinguished, huh? I think you enjoy the wisdom that comes with my age," Thad teased.

Billy laughed softly, the light banter making the moment even more intimate. "Maybe I do. It's part of your charm."

Thad smiled and took Billy's hand, leading him toward the bedroom. "Come on. Let's find somewhere more comfortable."

Billy followed eagerly, his heart racing with anticipation. Thad turned to face him as they entered the bedroom, his expression reflecting a deep, heartfelt connection.

"Are you sure about this?" Thad asked softly.

Billy nodded, his eyes locked onto Thad's. "I've never been more sure of anything."

"Then let's not waste any more time," Thad said, his voice husky with desire.

Thad leaned in, his lips brushing against Billy's ear as he whispered, "I want to feel every inch of you."

They came together in a passionate kiss, their hands exploring each other's bodies with newfound urgency. Thad's hands moved slowly, deliberately, as he unbuttoned Billy's shirt. Each button slipped through its hole teasingly, making Billy shiver with anticipation. As Thad slid the final button free, he gently pushed the shirt off Billy's shoulders, letting it fall to the floor in a whisper of fabric.

Thad's eyes lingered on the pearl choker adorning Billy's

neck, a symbol of delicate elegance amidst the heat of the moment. Slowly, his fingers traced the cool, smooth pearls, each one pressing lightly against Billy's skin, heightening the sensation. The simple yet intimate touch sent a shiver down Billy's spine, his breath catching as he felt Thad's fingertips glide over the choker, making every nerve in his body spark with desire. The pearls, cold against his flushed skin, contrasted with the warmth of Thad's touch, a sensation that deepened the connection between them. Thad's fingers moved with a tender and possessive sensuality, as if he memorized the feel of each pearl, each curve of Billy's neck, before his lips followed the path his fingers had traced, leaving a trail of kisses in their wake.

Billy followed suit, his hands trembling slightly as he lifted Thad's shirt over his head. He traced the lines of Thad's muscles, savoring his skin's firm, smooth texture. Thad's breath hitched as Billy's hands moved lower, working on Thad's belt, unbuckling it carefully, the sound of the metal clasp sparking in the quiet room. As each piece of clothing fell away, they stood together, bared in more ways than one. Billy's touch was eager, his desire overcoming any hesitation, their eyes meeting with an intensity that made the moment even more charged.

When Thad finally lifted Billy onto the bed, their bodies fit together as if they'd always belonged. They moved in sync, a dance of desire and tenderness, exploring each other with reverence.

As they made love, Billy realized this was where he was meant to be—with Thad, sharing something deeper and more meaningful than he had ever known.

Lying together, their bodies intertwined, Billy felt utterly immersed in the sensation of being so intimately connected.

Every touch, every kiss sent shivers of pleasure down his spine, making him feel as though he were in a dream. Thad's hands were gentle and firm, guiding him with a tenderness that filled his heart with love. Thad's presence was intoxicating, a blend of allure and intensity that ignited Billy's deepest desires. This man, who had captured his heart with a glance and caress, was enchanting.

When they finally collapsed, spent and satisfied, Billy looked into Thad's eyes and saw his feelings reflected.

"I love you, Thad," he whispered, his voice filled with emotion.

Thad's smile was radiant. "I love you too, Billy. And I promise, I'm not going anywhere."

Billy nestled closer, feeling the steady beat of Thad's heart against his chest. He felt truly at peace for the first time in a long while. He knew that whatever challenges lay ahead, they would face them together.

In the quiet of Thad's bedroom, Billy reflected on the night of firsts: the premiere of "Transcendence" at a Broadway theater, his coming to terms with Pierce, and now, his long-awaited union with Thad. He was exhausted yet in a state of ultimate bliss. With Thad by his side, Billy felt safe and cared for. Thad's apartment felt new and unfamiliar, but Billy thought he might finally find his home.

As they drifted off to sleep, wrapped in each other's arms, Billy couldn't help but smile. This was just the beginning of their story. As his eyes grew heavy, questions lingered: What did the future hold for their relationship? Was there even a future for them together, or was this just the culmination of a night of firsts?

Chapter 31

As with many dance and opera seasons, the same program was not offered each night. Instead, the individual numbers within a two-week run were rotated. This meant that Billy and Liam's piece, "Transcendence," was not performed every night. This rotation gave dancers a break from the routine of performing the same program each night and allowed Billy to avoid daily commuting into the city. This was beneficial since he also had his school's holiday concert to prepare for just days after his final performance in New York. Despite the stress of balancing responsibilities in two places, he found immense joy in sharing his work with audiences, fulfilling a lifelong dream.

But another dream was fulfilled, too. He and Thad had finally made love, and now Billy pondered the possibility of a more serious relationship. However, Thad hadn't shown interest in repeating their passionate night together during the remainder of the dance company's New York run, which caused Billy to doubt they had a future together. Their interactions seemed business-like and distant. While he cherished their passionate night and hoped it might lead to something more, even though he said he wasn't going anywhere, Thad's lack of interest in repeating that intimacy left Billy unsure about where they stood, especially now that the dance company's season had ended. He had given Thad what he needed: his piano piece, "Transcendence," and his heart. While he appreciated Thad's expertise as a music director and having his music in Marsha Morgan's current Broadway run, he wondered if Thad felt the same about his work as a teacher or understood what his upcoming holiday concert with his kids meant to him.

He desperately needed a break from the constant back-and-forth commuting into the city when he was also putting in a full day at school. That break was today, Sunday, with the final performance last night. He'd use this day to recover, especially with his school concert scheduled for Thursday.

The day dawned bright and clear as if the universe had decided to give Billy a cheery greeting card to start his new chapter. He was halfway through demolishing a bowl of cereal when his phone buzzed, announcing a plot twist to his long-awaited day off.

"Vik!" he answered.

"Good morning, sunshine!" Her greeting was like a trumpet's blaring fanfare.

Billy gagged, dislodging a bit of granola that had gotten stuck in his windpipe in reaction to Viktoria's greeting. "What's going on? Aren't you at work?"

"Yes, Billy, I'm at work." Muffled words sounded in the background. "Misty says hi."

"Tell her I said hi, too."

"It's happening, Billy. Happening now. Wally's being released, and we must get him from prison."

Billy had promised Viktoria that he would be there for both of them when Wally was released, but he hadn't expected it so soon. He cast off the idea for his day of rest. He'd recharge some other day.

"I'll come up to The Flambroidery, and we can leave from

there," Billy affirmed.

"We'll take my car, but I want you to drive; I'm too much of a mess to be behind the wheel."

"How much time do I have?" Billy asked.

"Oh, we've got a couple of hours. It's nearly ten o'clock, so we should leave the shop by noon."

Having some wiggle room, Billy decided to ride his bike, which he'd had no time for since his work in New York began. The day was mild for December, and he'd follow the chain of linked boardwalks from Beachside north to Asbury Park. It shouldn't take him more than forty-five minutes, an hour at best, and he could use the exercise.

As Billy pedaled through several shore towns, he re-called stories Viktoria had told him—stories she'd heard from old-timers about what gay life was like before Asbury Park be-came the upscale restaurant destination and high-priced lux-ury condo market it is today. Viktoria's voice echoed in his mind:

"Asbury Park back in the day was a haven if you were gay, a place where you could indeed be yourself. In the forties, fif-ties, and sixties, men could dress casually in bars—there was no need for the suit, tie, and hat that were mandatory in New York City mafia-controlled bars.

"There was one popular bar, The Blue Note. It was so popular that lines would stretch down the street with people waiting to get in. It had been a jazz club, catering exclusively to a straight clientele, but when the owners saw the potential, they made it a thriving gay piano bar, like La Péniche today.

"It was shut down for a while in the mid-sixties by the state's Alcohol Beverage Control (ABC) for catering to homo-sexuals. The agents said they knew it was a gay bar because the men wore too-tight jeans, turtleneck sweaters, floral-print pants, paisley shirts, sneakers and boots. When it reopened, the doorman had to run around the place to ensure that men weren't touching or kissing each other. Can you believe that? The locals, including the police and politicians, had a live-and-let-live attitude about the place and seldom, if ever, raided or harassed the customers."

Billy felt the crisp sea breeze against his face as he navigated towards The Flambroidery, grateful to live in more accepting times. He loved how the boards rumbled beneath his tires—a continuous theme with rhythmic variations inspired by the varied lengths and widths of planks as he crossed into each new beach town, the percussive vibrations echoing through his body. The only changes to the pattern involved crossing a drawbridge when an inlet got in the way, requiring him to ride over the welded wire mesh road surface, a seamless segue with its own unique thematic vibration. Viktoria's stories, in counterpoint with the music of the boards and bridges, deepened his connection to the history and evolution of the place, making his ride to the vibrant town even more meaningful.

Arriving at The Flambroidery, Billy locked his bike outside and walked into the shop, immediately enveloped by its lively atmosphere. A beacon of bright colors defined the shop's facade. The exterior's centerpiece was a sign depicting a sleek embroidery needle in shimmering metallic silver, standing tall and central. Instead of thread, an opulent feathered boa in vibrant gradient shades of fuchsia, teal, and gold spiraled playfully from the needle's eye. This lush creation, set against a striking oval backdrop that transitioned from deep purple to bright pink, perfectly captured the shop's flamboyant spirit.

Below the graphic, the shop's name, "The Flambroidery," was elegantly displayed in a playful script font, with white letters that shimmered subtly. Tiny tips of fiber optic cables embedded in the sign pulsated with glints of pinpoint lights that danced around the boa and needle, adding a touch of magic and glamour to the whimsical design. Inside, the store was a treasure trove of drag essentials, with walls covered in shimmering fabrics, feather boas, and sequined accessories. Mannequins dressed in extravagant costumes greeted customers at the entrance.

Ever dramatic, Viktoria opted for a slightly toned-down version of her usual extravagant attire. She wore simple black tights and a billowy white blouse, a respectful nod to something Judy or Liza might have worn in rehearsal. On the other hand, Misty Drizzle remained true to her over-the-top style, this time without the burdensome addition of her multilayered hoop skirt, which would never have fit into a Honda Fit. She chose a vibrant, multi-colored outfit with horizontal stripes, sequins, and a propellered beanie, bringing humor and lightness to the occasion.

Viktoria assisted a customer with a selection of wigs while Misty adjusted a feather boa on a mannequin. The shop buzzed with activity as customers browsed and chatted, their laughter blending with the upbeat music playing in the background.

"Hey, Billy!" Viktoria called out, spotting him at the door. "Just in time!"

Billy smiled and approached the counter. "Hey, Vik! Everything looks fantastic in here, as always."

"Thanks, darling," Viktoria replied, quickly hugging him. "We're just about to wrap up for the morning. How was your ride over?"

"Great, actually," Billy said, glancing around at the familiar, vibrant space. "I love how lively this place always is."

Misty joined them, her eyes sparkling with excitement. "Billy, it's so good to see you! We've got everything ready for Wally. He's going to be so happy."

Billy's heart swelled with anticipation. "I'm glad I could help."

Misty, taking complete control, called out to the handful of remaining customers, "Time to wrap it up, folks!" The customers quickly gathered their things. Viktoria grabbed a colorful bag filled with snacks and a bunch of helium-filled balloons they had purchased for Wally's release.

Billy took the keys to Viktoria's bright blue 2003 Honda Fit. Despite its age and the rust creeping along the bottom of the door frames, the car was filled with character, much like Viktoria herself. The interior was vibrant, with mismatched seat covers, a dashboard adorned with quirky trinkets, and small, colorful custom drag queen bobbleheads.

The trio squeezed into the car, with Billy somehow wedging himself into the driver's seat. Viktoria claimed the shotgun position, clutching a dislodged bobblehead dash ornament, while Misty was in the back, waging a losing battle against a flock of bobbing balloons. As they cruised down the road, the car's shocks groaning in protest, Billy wondered if Viktoria had even considered where Wally would fit in the sub-compact car. It was too bad rumble seats went out of fashion in the 1930s because one would have been helpful now.

The imposing gates loomed as they approached the Coastal State Correctional Facility, its massive dome prominent against the sky. If the Pantheon housed gods, beneath this dome lay the broken dreams of men, interrupted lives awaiting redemption, a repository of human frailty delicately balanced between justice and mercy.

Viktoria's excitement was palpable, her hands trembling slightly. She spotted Wally, a free man, walking towards them. Without waiting for the car to come to a complete stop, Viktoria jumped out.

"Wally!" she cried, rushing towards him with open arms, tears streaming down her face. "I can't believe you're finally free!"

Wally's face lit up with relief and joy as he saw his friends arriving. Misty and Billy followed, offering their congratulations and support. They helped Wally gather his belongings: a paper grocery bag filled with personal items and a pair of worn canvas sneakers.

"This is amazing," Wally said, his voice choked with emotion. "Thank you all so much for being here."

The backseat of the car was a small celebration waiting to happen, with balloons bobbing, a basket of snacks, and letters of encouragement. Wally's eyes widened in surprised delight as he realized their effort to make his release day special.

"You guys are the best," he said, a broad smile spreading across his face, feeling the support of his friends.

As they drove back, the conversation turned to Wally's plans for the future. He spoke of finding a job, reconnecting with family, and starting anew. Viktoria, Misty, and Billy listened intently, offering their support and advice.

Billy promised, "We'll help you every step of the way. You're not alone in this."

Viktoria nodded enthusiastically. "Absolutely. We're your cheerleaders, your support team, and your family."

Misty grinned, "And if you ever need a little sparkle in

your life, you know who to call."

The car was filled with laughter and camaraderie, their worries and uncertainties momentarily forgotten. Billy glanced in the rearview mirror and saw Wally looking out the window, taking in the sights of a new world full of possibilities. Surrounded by friends who believed in him, Billy knew Wally could face whatever challenges lay ahead, especially with the promise of a life shared with Viktoria.

Chapter 32

Billy was still riding high from the celebratory premiere of "Transcendence" and his new extended family in New York. Thankfully, he had recovered from his never-ending commute between his teaching job at Beachside Elementary School and rehearsals in New York. More time might be required to get over his run-in with Pierce Talon at his favorite restaurant. He was hopeful, however, that his late-night intervention with the chef would end his interference in Billy's life from now on. And, because of the agreement with Pierce to keep his distance, he could continue hanging out at his favorite restaurant, enjoying small talk at the bar and an intimate meal with friends whenever he was in the city, even though Pierce had taken possession of Curtain Call kitchen.

Yet, in a moment of unexpected clarity, Billy began to realize that Pierce's seemingly sociopathic behavior might have deeper roots. It dawned on him that Pierce's hypermasculine facade was less about dominance and more about survival—a necessary shield against his father's intolerance of his sexuality.

But Thad's absence weighed heavily on his heart. Since the final performance, there'd been no call, no text, no email—nothing. The silence was more than just a void; it was a growing wound, a reminder of the connection he feared was lost forever.

And while his obligations in New York were over, Billy wasn't done with performances yet. Tonight was his school's annual winter concert, and he needed to focus on his students and help them shine for their parents and his fellow teachers.

The school hallway between the music room and cafetorium was the staging area for easily distracted children. Outside the ill-conceived multifunction room that tried to be all things for all purposes—gym, cafeteria, auditorium, and failing at all three—stood Viktoria, albeit with a poor attitude at this moment. She had wanted to bring Wally to the concert to help, but Wally hadn't completely transitioned back into the world where he could feel at ease in public, so he opted to stay home.

For Billy's concert, Viktoria wore a Cinderella gown accented with a do-it-yourself boa, more craft than fashion, constructed out of snipped evergreen boughs and sprigs of holly held together with hot glue and ribbons. Unfortunately, with everything happening around Billy's New York performances and Wally's release from prison, little time was available to construct her costume correctly. Despite the lack of time, she had overworked it to the extent of weaponizing it. Even adding a strand of tiny, battery-operated twinkling lights failed to bring the holiday cheer she had imagined. Billy thought she had crucified a Christmas wreath from The Home Depot. The assemblage looked like a torture device from the Dark Ages, and the holly leaves pricked at Viktoria's neck, causing her to scratch involuntarily.

The itching increased as she became more frustrated with the task at hand. She fussed with the eighty fourth, fifth, and sixth graders who suddenly had no clue what it meant to assemble in a straight line or follow directions in the long hallway leading to the school's cafetorium. It was good that Viktoria read to prisoners rather than told stories to children during drag queen story hours. It wasn't that she couldn't stand children; she once was a child herself, though it was hard for her to remember at this moment. Right now, she had no patience for them.

"Billy, where are you? Come out here this instant and corral your children. Now!" In her frustration, she swooped one end of the boa and tossed it over her opposite shoulder, embedding tiny leaf holly spikes into her throat and barely missing two students nearby. The children, at least the few paying attention to her, giggled at the sight, and Viktoria nearly lost it completely.

Billy stepped out of the music room, where the line of kids ended. Each child snapped to attention as he passed by, creating a reverse domino effect. Viktoria watched in awe as the chorus assembled, poised to advance onto the stage and fill the waiting risers.

Viktoria entered through the cafetorium door and sat beside Billy's dad in the front row. Billy had worked with Mr. Whitaker, the school custodian, for an hour after school to arrange an army of folding chairs into a suitable formation for the two hundred or so audience members expected to attend. Anticipation grew among the parents and fellow teachers, and a hush swept over the crowd, like the silence that descends on an audience just before the curtain rises on a sold-out Broadway hit.

The stage curtains parted, spasming along a contrary-minded traverse rod in desperate need of lubrication and a pep talk, revealing eighty smiling faces. Viktoria marveled at how cherub-like and neatly framed the chorus looked on stage, so not the wiggly, wired, and ready-to-warble brood she had experienced just moments before in the hall. The audience went wild upon seeing the children, especially the parents and grandparents. It was as if they had been reunited with loved ones after years apart, even though they had dropped their kids off thirty minutes earlier.

The principal came to the front of the audience and welcomed parents and guests to Beachside Elementary's winter concert. She thanked the parents for having such talented children and sharing them with her and the school. She made a few more announcements about the upcoming winter recess and the annual book fair in January. She then introduced Billy as he entered through the side door, acknowledged the audience, and sat at the piano, which had been wheeled in from his classroom and positioned in front of the stage apron.

The program included a diverse collection of songs the chorus had worked on since September. And as best he could, and considering the separation of church and state in public education, he managed to produce a program that embraced the season, both culturally and spiritually, with familiar tunes and beloved melodies from Hanukkah, Christmas, Kwanzaa and Yule. And yet, in some tricky and magical way, it didn't offended people's religious beliefs. It was like decking the halls with dreidels, holly, ivy and gilt.

The performance concluded with a rousing rendition of "Jingle Bells." For the final refrain, Billy stood up from the piano, his left hand continuing to hammer out a rhythmic bass line so that the whole thing wouldn't fall apart, and turned to the audience, gesturing for them to sing as their buoyant children descended the staircases from each side of the apron and joined their families in celebration. Sweet chaos.

The principal returned to speak to the crowd once she could get their attention, acknowledging Billy's hard work in putting together the concert. She thanked the children for their efforts and wished parents a happy holiday season. People began to trickle out of the cafetorium as Billy collected music sheets and discarded programs. Viktoria did her best to help without the boa inflicting more damage to her throat.

Billy took a moment to gather his thoughts as he approached Viktoria, who was still fussing with the remnants of her DIY costume. He knew he had to thank her for her help, but he also wanted to share something that had been on his mind.

"Vik, you know, tonight's concert—it's more than just a performance for me," he began, glancing around the now empty cafetorium. "When I plan these events, I think a lot about the kids and their families. I want every child to see themselves reflected in what we do here."

Viktoria, momentarily pausing her struggle with the holly-studded boa, looked at Billy with curiosity. "What do you mean, Billy?"

Billy sighed, choosing his words carefully. "I've always believed that if a child doesn't see their culture, their celebrations, their stories represented, or being called by their names, it's like telling them they don't exist. I never want any of my students to feel that way."

Viktoria's expression softened as she took in his words. "So, you're saying that by using their names and honoring their cultures and stories, you're giving them a sense of belonging, a way to mark their place here and in the world?"

Billy's passion was evident in his voice. "Exactly! Especially their names," he emphasized. "Every child deserves to be called by their name, not to go nameless walking these hallways. It's a way of showing them that their backgrounds and identities are valued. Every child deserves to be on our stage and experience something that resonates with them, something that lets them know they belong here."

Viktoria smiled, her frustration melting away. "Billy, that's beautiful. And it's clear tonight that your kids *did* feel that. They were glowing up there."

"Thanks, Vik," Billy said. "It's a small thing, but if it helps them feel seen and valued, it's worth all the effort."

As Viktoria adjusted her boa one last time, she looked at Billy with newfound respect. "You're doing good work, Billy. Keep making those kids feel like they're part of the world."

Billy nodded, grateful for her support. "I will, Vik. I will. And, Vik?"

"Yes, Billy?"

"Why don't you remove that boa before you do permanent damage to your neck?"

Viktoria bristled, her eyes widening in disbelief. "Excuse me? I'm beginning to wonder if you understand style at all. I'm so disappointed in you, Billy." With that, she side-eyed Billy, moved to another section of seats, and continued picking up stray programs and trash, tossing them into the large, wheeled trashcans by the food service windows. Once done, she stiletto-toed back to Billy and offered him a cheek. He responded with an air kiss as she grabbed her clutch and slipped into her vegan fur coat. She moved to the double doors leading to the now nearly empty parking lot. But before pushing against the crash bar, and without turning around, she raised her right hand in a refined gesture and, with a subtle twist from the wrist, produced a royal wave to whoever might be watching. Her effort exuded a pseudo-sophistication without veering into excessive enthusiasm, something entirely alien to Viktoria's typically flippant and flamboyant personality. Her hip hit the crash bar, and she left; a glittery cloud of powdery snow cloaked her in mystery as she merged with the night, fading from view.

The place had now emptied. Billy and Mr. Whitaker placed the folding chairs on several long, wheeled caddies for storage; once on the racks, the aligned chairs resembled a formation of troops poised for their next deployment. Billy helped push the racks into the storage bays under the stage. He thanked Mr. Whitaker for all his help and said goodbye as the custodian went off to secure the building for the night. Billy picked up his music folder from the piano. As he turned to leave, he noticed a solitary figure wearing a navy double-breasted topcoat standing in a doorway at the far end of the room. He held a dozen yellow roses in his hand.

Acknowledgements

Writing *The Object of His Affection* has been an emotionally re-warding journey. What began as an exploration of personal truths grew into a novel in which fictional characters express universal themes of life, love, and ambition while staying true to their unique experiences. The story delves into the power of music, the courage to pursue one's passion, and the complexity of relationships—especially when the past threatens to overshadow the present.

This novel would not have reached its potential without the unwavering support of my creative community. To my beta readers—Kristyn Hegener Kamps, Barbara Ryan Woolley, and Amy Simon—thank you for your insightful feedback, encouragement, and patience. Your thoughtful critiques were invaluable in refining this story.

I am profoundly grateful to my husband, Doug Hunter, whose love and encouragement sustained me through the highs and lows of this process. Thank you for always believing in me.

I also want to thank Gotham Writers Workshop, my editor, Ben Obler, and Synthetic Prophetc for providing the space and guidance to hone my craft. Your support pushed me to dig deeper, risk vulnerability on the page, and trust the creative process.

What began as a memoir soon evolved into a work of fiction, as I found that the story demanded more freedom to explore its themes. While it retains many personal experiences and emotions, fiction allowed me to delve deeper into these truths with greater nuance and complexity. After all, fiction often reveals insights that real life cannot. My hope is that readers discover a part of themselves within these pages, just as I have.

Thank you for being part of this journey.

—Donald Proffit